# LAST DANCE

## OTHER BOOKS BY MELODY CARLSON:

### Carter House Girls series

*Mixed Bags (Book One)*
*Stealing Bradford (Book Two)*
*Homecoming Queen (Book Three)*
*Viva Vermont! (Book Four)*
*Lost in Las Vegas (Book Five)*
*New York Debut (Book Six)*
*Spring Breakdown (Book Seven)*

### Books for Teens

The Secret Life of Samantha McGregor series
Diary of a Teenage Girl series
TrueColors series
Notes from a Spinning Planet series
Degrees series
*Piercing Proverbs*
By Design series

### Women's Fiction

*These Boots Weren't Made for Walking*
*On This Day*
*An Irish Christmas*
*The Christmas Bus*
*Crystal Lies*
*Finding Alice*
*Three Days*

### Grace Chapel Inn Series, *including*

*Hidden History*
*Ready to Wed*
*Back Home Again*

*carter house girls*

# LAST DANCE

# MELODY CARLSON

**ZONDERVAN®**

ZONDERVAN.com/
AUTHORTRACKER
*follow your favorite authors*

ZONDERVAN

*Last Dance*
Copyright © 2010 by Melody Carlson

Requests for information should be addressed to:
Zondervan, *Grand Rapids, Michigan* 49530

Library of Congress Cataloging-in-Publication Data

Carlson, Melody.
        Last dance / Melody Carlson.
            p. cm.—(Carter House girls ; bk. 8)
        Summary: As graduation and last good-byes approach, the Carter House girls
    make prom plans and find themselves in heated competion for the limelight in a
    Mother's Day fashion show.
        ISBN  978-0-310-71495-8 (softcover)
        [1. Interpersonal relations—Fiction. 2. Boardinghouses—Fiction. 3. Conduct of
    life—Fiction. 4. High schools—Fiction. 5. Schools—Fiction. 6. Christian life—Fiction.]
    I. Title.
        PZ7.C216637Las 2010
        [Fic]—dc22                                                    2009049549

*Interior design: Christine Orejuela-Winkelman*
*Composition: Carlos Eluterio Estrada*

*Printed in the United States of America*

10 11 12 13 14 15 16 17 18 /DCI/ 20 19 18 17 16 15 14 13 12 11 10 9 8 7 6 5 4 3 2

# LAST DANCE

**"I can't believe** it's only six weeks until graduation." Kriti groaned, then turned her attention back to the history book in her lap.

"If anyone doesn't need to worry about graduation, it's you, Kriti." Taylor reached for the fruit platter. "You've got it made it the shade, girl."

Kriti gave Taylor a half smile. But DJ knew Kriti wasn't concerned about graduating—that was a given. Kriti was obsessed with getting top honors at Crescent Cove High, even more so since she recently received her letter of acceptance from Harvard.

"Hopefully none of the Carter House girls need worry about graduation." Grandmother scanned the girls around the breakfast table. "I can only assume that all of you are maintaining your grades."

"Of course," DJ assured her. Naturally, she wasn't going to admit what *kind* of grades they all were maintaining. And to be fair, DJ had actually been applying herself to her studies for most of the year. In fact, since returning to classes after spring break, it seemed that all the girls had gotten more diligent about school … and life in general. How long this sense of serious sobriety would last (both figuratively and literally) was anyone's guess. But DJ was not complaining.

"Here's a thought." Eliza's eyes lit up. "Instead of focusing on how long it is until graduation, why not focus on the fact we have only two weeks until prom."

"Like it's possible to forget," DJ tossed back at her. "Everywhere you turn in school there's a glossy, glitzy poster in your face—and half of them belong to Miss Eliza Wilton."

"So you've probably noticed the rest of them belong to Madison Dormont and Haley Callahan," retorted Eliza. "And I would really appreciate it if the Carter House girls would back me in my campaign a little more." She looked hopefully at Grandmother. "Don't you agree, Mrs. Carter? Shouldn't we all support each other like a family?"

Grandmother gave DJ a look of frustration. She'd already questioned why DJ had no interest in running for prom queen, but DJ had adamantly answered, "No way!" Grandmother now smiled and nodded. "Yes, of course, Eliza, all the girls should be perfectly willing to help you. It would be wonderful to have a Carter House girl as prom queen."

"Great. I'm going to have a campaign strategy meeting Sunday night and I'd like all of you to attend." Eliza beamed. "And it will be catered."

DJ suppressed the urge to say "Whooptie do!"

"And I thought this weekend might be a good time for everyone to model their gowns," Eliza continued, this time aiming her words at Grandmother. "We can have a fashion critique night with Mrs. Carter as judge. Doesn't that sound like fun?"

*Fun like a root canal*, DJ thought.

"Not everyone's dress will be ready this weekend," Rhiannon protested.

Eliza nodded knowingly in DJ's direction. "Yes, so I've heard. Some girls seem to be dragging their heels—as if they think a fairy godmother is going to show up and wave her magic wand ... right, DJ?"

DJ laughed. "Yeah, that sounds like a good idea to me."

Eliza had been pestering everyone about prom dresses for the past couple of weeks—ever since her mom had shipped her a beautiful gown from Paris, which she'd already sent out for alterations. So far only Kriti had caved to the pressure, allowing Eliza to drag her out formal shopping last weekend. Kriti probably gave in just to shut Eliza up so she could study without interruption.

"But what will you wear if your fairy godmother doesn't show?" continued Eliza. "Your soccer uniform perhaps?"

DJ rolled her eyes. "Give me a break, Eliza. I'll have a dress in time for the prom."

"I can only imagine what kind of lame dress you'll manage to dig up at the last minute. And please, don't go to one of those rental places." Eliza made an expression that strangely resembled Grandmother. "Honestly, DJ, why do you insist on waiting until the last minute for anything that's remotely related to fashion? It's like you get some kind of thrill out of being difficult."

DJ just shrugged and picked up her coffee cup. She was tempted to remind Eliza that she wasn't the only one without a prom dress. But what difference would it make? Once Eliza got stuck on something like this, she was like a pit bull. Sure, she might be a pit bull dressed in a pink Marc Jacobs jacket and lip gloss—but a pit bull all the same. Lately DJ had begun to suspect this fixation on prom was simply Eliza's cover-up ... a way to conceal the troubles that lay beneath. Even the fact that she and

Lane had recently begun dating felt like a distraction device. Like Eliza was so caught up in creating her "perfect" little world that she never had time to think about her traumatic kidnapping incident in Palm Beach a couple weeks ago. Like it had never even happened. And, according to Rhiannon (Eliza's roommate), Eliza had lied to Grandmother, saying that she'd informed her parents about the whole thing when she really hadn't.

"FYI," Taylor announced lightly, "DJ and I will be going prom dress shopping this weekend." She glanced at DJ. "Right, Roomie?"

DJ shrugged, then noticed that Grandmother was eyeing her with interest.

"That sounds like a good plan, DJ," Grandmother said. "Just don't forget we have modeling class on Saturday morning. You girls all know that the Mother's Day fashion show is only three weeks away, but you might not know it's completely sold out. It could well be Crescent Cove's biggest fund-raising event ever. Just this week, Mayor Daschall told me how proud he is of the Carter House girls. He wants the newspaper to do a feature article on you the week before the fashion show. He's actually calling you girls the future first citizens of the next generation."

DJ held back the groan that was threatening to erupt as her grandmother droned on about how the Carter House girls were such fine examples. Was the mayor as delusional as Grandmother? Or were they all in deep, deep denial? Even so, DJ felt a tiny stab of pity for the old woman. She actually seemed to care about the girls … and she'd been a pretty good sport these past few weeks—especially in light of what they'd all gone through during spring break. DJ had honestly expected Grandmother to send all the girls packing once they'd gotten home. But, other than a rather lengthy lecture and stern warning about abiding by the house rules, she hadn't. As a result, DJ had been trying to be more positive and cooperative lately. But hearing the mayor's praise of the girls made DJ want to scream. If only he knew the truth.

As Grandmother wound down her little pep talk, Casey quietly excused herself. It seemed that everyone at the table was subdued now. Perhaps they all felt a bit of guilt. *Future first citizens of the next generation ...* with the kinds of problems these girls had experienced this past year? It was psychotic, DJ thought.

And, unless DJ was mistaken, their problems weren't over with yet. She watched as Casey silently exited the dining room. It felt like Casey was trying to slip beneath the radar, like she had something to hide. DJ honestly didn't know what to make of her anymore. Despite the fact that Casey had retracted the confession she'd made at Palm Beach, DJ still had a feeling that it could be true.

Oh, she knew it made no sense, but she still had this nagging fear that Casey really could be pregnant. And yet Casey had firmly denied this possibility. She'd explicitly told DJ that she'd been mistaken—false alarm, no harm no foul, end of story. And after that she refused to even discuss it. And, really, why would Casey lie? DJ just needed to let it go and forget about it.

Of course, it didn't help matters that Casey had started dating Seth again. Oh, like the other Carter House girls, she'd definitely calmed down her social life these past few weeks, but DJ had been disappointed to see Casey and Seth still together. Didn't Casey get that Seth was bad news? Didn't she see the way he treated her, how he took her for granted, and how he was after only one thing? Still, just like Taylor had hinted more than once, maybe DJ needed to back off. "All you can do is warn her and wait," Taylor had said. "You start pushing her and she'll probably just go in the other direction." And Taylor should know, since she'd been there herself not so very long ago.

Just the same, DJ found it hard to give up on her old friend, and that's why she excused herself and hurried off in hopes of catching Casey. She'd invite her to shop for prom dresses. But Casey had already grabbed her bag and was on her way back down.

"Hey, Case," DJ said as she casually blocked the way, "why don't you come shopping with Taylor and me on Saturday?"

Casey's brow creased. "Well, for one thing, I'm just about flat broke."

"But I thought you were going to the prom with Seth — don't you need a dress?"

"I do. But Rhiannon offered to help me with it."

"Oh . . . that's nice of her."

"Maybe . . ." Casey's scowl deepened. "In exchange I have to go to youth group with her for the next three weeks."

DJ grinned. Score points for Rhiannon!

"Yeah, it figures that would make you happy."

DJ heard the other girls coming out of the dining room. They'd be heading for the stairs and their last-minute grabs before school.

"It's just that I care about you," DJ said quickly. "And I'd really like to talk to you — "

"Later." Casey cut her off, pushed past her, and hurried down the stairs.

*Keep praying for her*, DJ told herself as she headed for her room. Maybe that was all she could do. Just keep her mouth shut and pray. Really, what was so hard about that? And maybe she was making something out of nothing. Just let it go.

"Sorry to force you into prom dress shopping," Taylor said as she came into their room. She paused in front of the closet mirror, fluffing her hair and retouching her lip gloss. "It just seemed like the best way to silence Miss Eliza. Besides, she's sort of right. The longer we put it off, the less we'll have to choose from."

"Yeah, I suppose shopping's just a necessary evil."

Taylor laughed. "Someday, you're going to look back on these times of enforced fashion assistance and realize how much you needed me."

DJ made a face. "Yeah, like the next time I'm dribbling the soccer ball toward the winning goal, I'll pause to flip my hair and say to myself, 'Oh, yeah, that stylish Taylor Mitchell, where would I be without her today?'"

Taylor made a face as she closed the lid on her lip gloss. "Hey, there's nothing wrong with being an attractive athlete."

"Especially if you're going for product endorsements ... which I don't see coming my way anytime soon." DJ slung the strap of her bag over a shoulder and reached for the doorknob.

"Were you talking to Casey on the stairs?" Taylor asked quietly.

"Trying to." DJ shook her head. "I just wish she'd open up."

"She will when she's ready."

DJ closed the bedroom door behind them. "I tried to talk her into shopping with us on Saturday."

"Good idea, except I hear Rhiannon's making her dress."

"You guys talking about Casey?" Rhiannon asked as the three merged at the top of the stairs.

DJ glanced around to see if anyone else was within earshot.

"They're all downstairs," Rhiannon assured her.

"It's just that I'm worried about Casey," DJ admitted. "It's obvious that something's wrong. She tries to hide it, but it looks like she's unhappy."

13

Rhiannon nodded. "She definitely seems different. I thought maybe she was depressed about school ... she told me her grades have slipped, but she said she was working on it. And Kriti offered to help her."

"Maybe that's all it is ..." DJ tried to sound hopeful. "Just her grades."

"Anyway, I made her promise to come to youth group"— Rhiannon grinned—"in trade for her prom dress. Seemed like a good deal to me."

"And brilliant." DJ reached out to give her a high five.

"Maybe." Taylor didn't look convinced. "Just don't forget the old adage about leading a horse to water ... just because you drag her there doesn't mean she'll drink."

"If she's thirsty, she might."

DJ jangled her keys. "We better get going or we'll be late."

As DJ drove the three of them to school, she was still thinking about Casey. Maybe Rhiannon was right that Casey was simply worried about grades and graduation. And she probably should be. Yet, it just felt there was something else going on. For one thing, it seemed obvious that Casey had been avoiding DJ. Every day since spring break, Casey had ridden to school with Eliza. Besides that, Casey had quit soccer—and right before play-offs too. She'd claimed it was because of a reinjury to her knee, although DJ had never heard of this mysterious injury before. And she'd never seen Casey take a bad hit, plus she never limped or anything. Not that DJ had questioned Casey's story. She knew by then that, although Casey was acting all quiet and introverted, her fuse was short and she could explode at the slightest provocation. DJ did not care to provoke her.

Despite DJ's concern for Casey, she had never mentioned the Palm Beach confession to anyone—not even Conner, and she told him almost everything. And maybe that was a moot point now since Casey had insisted it had been a mistake. But why did DJ have such a hard time letting it go?

"What a gorgeous day," Rhiannon observed as they went up the front steps of the school.

DJ squinted up for one last glance at the brilliant blue sky before they went inside. "I feel a major case of spring fever coming on."

"Too bad we're stuck indoors all day." Taylor frowned as she removed her oversized shades.

"Hey, why don't we meet outside in the courtyard for lunch," DJ suggested as they were about to part ways.

"Sounds great," Taylor said as she turned away. "See ya then."

DJ was heading for the English department when she spotted Casey and decided to invite her to join them for an outdoor lunch. Pressing through a crowd of students, DJ suddenly realized that Casey was talking to Seth. And not just talking-talking either. They seemed to be in the thick of an intense conversation. DJ was about to turn away and give them their privacy when she saw Seth grab Casey firmly by her upper arm—and then he gave her a hard shake.

DJ couldn't stop herself. The next instant she was standing defensively by Casey's side. "What's going on here?" She directed this question to Seth.

"None of your business," he snapped back.

Casey nodded, but her eyes looked troubled. "It's okay."

"It doesn't look okay," DJ persisted. "I just saw Seth grab and shake you."

"Really," Casey insisted. "It's okay."

"And it's none of your business anyway." Seth glared at DJ.

DJ took a step closer to Seth. "Actually, it is my business. Casey is my friend. And if I thought you were abusing her, I wouldn't just sit around and watch."

"I'm not abusing her." He forced a smile now. "We were just playing around. Lighten up, DJ."

"Yeah," Casey added. "Lighten up."

DJ didn't know what to do. She just looked from one to the other, and then the bell rang. "Maybe you guys need to lighten up too," she said evenly. Then she turned and walked away. And although she was trying to act confident and slightly nonchalant, she felt shaken and unsettled. What had really been going on just then? And if Seth felt comfortable treating Casey like that when lots of people were around, what might he do when they were alone? Despite Seth's claim that it was none of her business, DJ knew that she was going to make it her business. And before the sun went down tonight, she and Casey were going to sit down and talk.

2

LAST Dance

AS IT turned out, the sun went down and came up again, and still DJ had been unable to corner Casey for a conversation. Now it was Friday night and it seemed that all the Carter House girls had plans to go out. DJ and Taylor were going with Conner and Harry to the Friday night art walk in town. Rhiannon was helping Bradford at his mom's gallery. Eliza and Kriti were headed for New York, staying at Kriti's house, then going with Lane and Josh to a Broadway show and late dinner.

"So what are you and Seth up to tonight?" DJ asked Casey after she finally managed to track her down in the library, of all places. Okay, she had her books out like she was studying, but DJ had her suspicions. It seemed more like a convenient hideout—a way to avoid DJ.

Casey stacked her books neatly and reached for her bag. "Just a movie," she said casually.

"What movie?"

"I'm not sure." She looked at her watch. "But he should be here any minute."

DJ moved toward the window that faced the street and looked out. "He's not here yet," she informed her.

"Oh." Casey drummed her fingers on the stacked books.

"I want to talk to you, Casey."

"About what?" Casey looked uneasy.

DJ thought for a moment. She knew she should be careful. "First of all, I'm sorry I kind of butted in on you and Seth yesterday. I didn't mean to intrude."

"That's okay."

"It's just that it caught me by surprise."

"Really, we were just playing around. No big deal."

"But that's not the only thing, Case." DJ glanced out the window again, then turned to Casey. "It just feels like you've pushed me away. Like we're not even friends anymore."

"We're friends."

"But we never talk."

"I've been busy, DJ. Uber-busy."

"I know. We all are. But that's never kept us from talking before. It feels like you're avoiding me."

"That's crazy. Why would I avoid you?" Casey looped the handle of her bag over her shoulder, like she was ready to bolt.

"I don't know. But I just thought it might help to talk."

"Except that Seth will be here any—"

"I'm watching for him. He's *not* here."

"Yeah, but—"

"What's going on with you, Casey?" DJ implored. "Is it something between you and Seth? Is he treating you badly?"

"I don't know why you're always accusing him of that."

"I'm not accusing anyone of—"

"You are too. It's like you hate him, DJ. It's like you think you're better than him. And you don't even know him. Not like I do."

"Well, obviously."

"See!" Casey pointed her finger. "There you go, making insinuations."

"I'm not making—"

"Yes, you are. You think the worst of him. And that means you think the worst of me. And if that's how you think, how are we supposed to be friends?"

DJ didn't know what to say.

"Seth loves me, DJ."

DJ blinked. "He loves you?"

"Yes! Why is that so hard to believe?"

She shrugged. "It just didn't look very loving when he shook you like that."

"See, there you go jumping to conclusions again."

"I know what I saw, Casey. That was not a loving thing to do."

"Who died and made you the expert on love?"

DJ sighed. This was not going the way she'd planned. "Look, Casey, I don't claim to be an expert on anything. And maybe I'm all wrong about Seth. In fact, I hope I am. But I still want to be your friend, okay? I want you to be able to talk to me . . . you know, if you ever need to. That's all I'm saying. Do you get that?"

Casey nodded, but her expression was doubtful.

"I'm sorry if I stepped on your toes. You know me, Case, I'm not a great diplomat. I usually just call it the way I see it."

"I know." Casey sniffed with indignation. "But sometimes the way you call it hurts."

"I'm sorry." DJ turned and looked out the window in time to see a car pulling up. "And it looks like Seth's here anyway."

Before DJ could even turn around, Casey was gone. DJ stood watching out the window. Casey hadn't waited for Seth to come up to the house. And for all DJ knew, maybe he never came up to the house. In fact, he didn't even get out of the car; he just sat there waiting in the driver's seat. Casey was barely in the car when he took off. How gallant.

DJ sat down in the old leather chair at the desk and considered the situation. Why was it that someone like Casey, someone who grew up in a church-going Christian home with a strong father figure, could settle for so little in a guy? And why was it that Casey was willing to be treated the way that DJ suspected Seth treated her? Was it simply a case of low self-esteem? Or was she some sort of masochist? What was going on in Casey's head?

"Hey," called Taylor. "I've been looking all over for you. Are you still on for the art walk tonight?"

"Of course." DJ slowly stood.

"Something wrong?"

"No, I just had a little chat with Casey." DJ had already told Taylor about the grabbing/shaking incident at school. Taylor hadn't even been surprised.

"Didn't go too well?"

"I'm sure you can imagine. I probably said everything you told me not to say."

"Sometimes people can only see what they want to see. Take it from me, I know this personally."

"I suppose . . . but I just wanted Casey to know I'm here for her . . . if she needs to talk."

"I'm sure she knows that already, DJ."

"I'm not so sure. And besides, I think I managed to thoroughly offend her—by dissing her boyfriend."

"Well, you tried. Anyway, Harry just called and he wanted to know if we were okay to get dinner first. He said that he and Conner are starving and if they don't eat before the art walk, they will perish."

DJ grinned. "No problem. I'm with them."

Taylor called Harry back and within minutes the guys arrived in Harry's Jeep. But, unlike Seth, both these guys came to the front door and both of them opened the car doors for the girls. And, although DJ knew it was only a gesture, she also knew that it was more than just a surface thing. And she appreciated it.

"You know what still amazes me?" Taylor said as the four of them were strolling down Main Street toward Bradford's mom's gallery and their final stop on the art walk.

"No, what?" ventured DJ.

"That we can have fun like this" — Taylor grinned — "without alcohol and stupid partying."

Harry nodded. "And no worries about getting dragged into City Hall and being booked for underage drinking."

"And no hangovers." Conner jabbed Harry with his elbow. "I still remember how wiped out you got on that ski trip to Vermont. You were in bad shape, man."

Harry laughed. "Yeah, can't say I miss that."

"Me neither," added Taylor.

"As for me," DJ said, "I never liked the taste of alcohol in the first place. And I always hated what I saw it doing to my friends."

"Hey, that looks like Seth's car." Conner pointed to a small red car crossing an intersection on Main Street.

"I thought they were at a movie." DJ studied the sports car as it zipped out of sight. "But they're going the wrong way."

"Looks like they're headed for the beach," Taylor observed as they paused in front of the Mockingbird Gallery.

"Anyone's guess as to why they're going there," Harry said lightly as he opened the plate-glass door, then waited until the girls went inside.

DJ let out a frustrated sigh. She had no doubts about what Harry was insinuating. And, although it made her mad to hear him say it, she knew that it probably was true. And, really, why should it surprise her? Everyone knew what Seth was like. Everyone except Casey, that is. Or maybe DJ was wrong. Maybe Casey knew exactly who Seth was ... but maybe she just didn't care.

"Hey, it's about time you guys showed up," said Rhiannon as she held out a platter of cheese and crackers to them. "I've been watching for you."

"We saved the best for last," Taylor said as she popped a piece of cheese into her mouth.

"Well, move around and act interested," Rhiannon said quietly. "Gabrielle is feeling a little blue that more people didn't show up."

"Maybe I don't have to act," Taylor told her. "Maybe I *am* interested."

Rhiannon beamed. "Great. And if I show you a piece that you buy, Gabrielle promised me a commission."

"So show me what you think is good." Taylor nodded toward Harry and, putting on airs, said, "Come on, dahling, let's do some art shopping. Perhaps we'll find a little something for Mother's Day."

"Brilliant idea," agreed Harry in a perfect British accent. "I'm sure my mum would appreciate a nice bit of art."

Several people in the gallery watched as Rhiannon led the handsome couple around. DJ suppressed a giggle as Harry continued in his Brit accent and Taylor looked at paintings that had to be beyond her budget.

"Serious shoppers, eh?" Bradford chuckled as he joined Conner and DJ.

"For your mom's sake, let's hope so," DJ said.

And, as it turned out, Harry and Taylor each made a purchase. Harry bought a hand-carved wooden bowl and Taylor got her mom a beautiful hand-thrown ceramic pitcher. "It's called raku," she explained to DJ. "Rhiannon said that means it was fired using an outdoor pit."

"It's gorgeous," DJ told her. "Every time you turn it, I see a different color."

"I can gift wrap these for you guys," Rhiannon offered, "if you're not in a hurry."

So while they waited, DJ wandered around the gallery again. She wondered what it would feel like to be buying her mom a Mother's Day gift. She couldn't actually remember buying a Mother's Day gift. She remembered her dad got Mom a toaster oven once and said it was from both of them. But when DJ saw Mom's disappointment in the appliance, she privately confessed that it hadn't been her choice. After the divorce, money had been tight, so DJ had made homemade cards and served breakfast in bed with flowers from the yard, and her mom had always seemed appreciative. And then she was killed in the car wreck … and DJ never got a chance to get her anything really nice. DJ stood admiring a small seascape painting. It was by a local painter and the scene looked familiar.

"That's pretty, isn't it?" Conner said as he came to stand beside her.

DJ nodded, swallowing the lump in her throat. "I was just thinking it's the kind of thing my mom would've loved."

Conner reached for her hand and gave it a squeeze. "You miss her sometimes, don't you?"

She nodded again. "Yeah … it usually catches me by surprise."

"I bet your grandmother misses her too."

DJ considered this. "Yeah ... you're probably right." She took in a deep breath. "You know, I'll bet my grandmother would like this painting."

"So ..." Bradford joined them, rubbing his hands together like a hungry salesman. "Can I interest you in this lovely acrylic? It's small but well done. And the artist is dead, so it's probably worth a lot."

DJ turned and looked at him. "Actually, I think I'd like to buy it."

"Really?" He blinked. "I mean, I wasn't seriously trying to get you —"

"I don't have the cash on me, but if your mom could hold it for a couple of days, I'll get some money from my savings on Monday."

"Yeah, sure, if you really want it, DJ."

"I do."

He reached out and shook her hand. "It's a deal."

DJ had no idea how Grandmother would react to this slightly extravagant gift, not to mention the fact that DJ would have to go into her college savings to purchase it, but DJ knew it was something she wanted to do.

Gabrielle left the older couple she'd been talking with and came over to join DJ and Conner and the others. "You kids," she said happily. "I'm so glad you came by tonight. And Bradford tells me that you're not just window-shopping either."

"You have some beautiful pieces here," Taylor told her.

"Thank you. It's so refreshing to see the younger generation with an appreciation for the arts." She smiled as Rhiannon came out with the wrapped and neatly bagged gifts, handing one to Taylor and one to Harry. "And dear Rhiannon, you've been such a help to me tonight." Gabrielle gave Rhiannon a big hug. "You kids are always welcome in my gallery!"

"And DJ wants to buy the Saltzer seascape," Bradford proudly informed his mom.

Gabrielle looked genuinely surprised. "Oh, DJ, you have an excellent eye for art. And, really, that piece is a bargain. Andrew Saltzer died a couple of years ago. This is one of the last paintings he did. I only acquired it last week."

DJ nodded. "That's what Bradford said."

"I told DJ we could hold it for her until Monday," Bradford explained.

"Certainly." Gabrielle grasped DJ's hand, giving it a squeeze. "I'm happy to do that. Thank you."

"Thank you," DJ told her.

"Are you kids going over to hear the music at the coffeehouse tonight?" Gabrielle asked. "Or maybe it's not your style of music."

"Who's playing?" Taylor asked with interest.

"Ben's Blue Boys," Gabrielle told them. "Ben's an old friend. They play a West Coast style of jazz. Sort of like Coltrane sound."

"Sounds good to me." Taylor turned to the others. "I'm in."

And so the six of them headed down the street to McHenry's Coffee House, where they snagged the last available table and enjoyed jazz and coffee and each other's company. It was really a great evening. But then DJ noticed a girl with short strawberry-blond hair, and for a moment she thought it was Casey. She felt disappointed when it wasn't. She wondered what Casey was doing right now. And whatever it was, wouldn't she be having more fun if she were here with them? Why didn't she get it?

3

LAST DANCE

"I have a surprise for everyone," Grandmother announced after the girls quieted down in the third-story ballroom where they had just convened for modeling practice. She looked toward the door behind them, then waved her hand as if to invite someone in. "Our favorite designer—Dylan Marceau is here!"

Everyone turned to see Dylan stride into the room like a celebrity. The girls all stood and clapped as he joined Grandmother in front.

"And I'm happy to see that my favorite models are here." Dylan smiled as he scanned the group. "As well as some new faces."

Grandmother smiled. "Yes, we invited a few more of the local girls to join us for the Mother's Day fashion show. Besides the eight girls at your New York debut, we have an additional four. Will you girls please stand when I say your names?" She glanced at her little cheat sheet. "Ariel Buford ... Jolene Kranz ... Tina Clark ... Madison Dormont. I thought it might be nice to have an even dozen."

"Very nice." Dylan nodded.

27

DJ wasn't inclined to agree. At least when it came to Madison and Tina. Those two girls still felt like trouble. But DJ was determined to do her best to get along. And if any catfights broke out, she would not be in the middle of them.

Dylan explained that the girls would be modeling the same line that they'd modeled during Fashion Week. "I apologize that it's not the new spring line, but I must keep that top secret until fall."

"But at least it will be new to Crescent Cove," Grandmother pointed out. "And we are so appreciative to have Dylan honor us like this."

"It's *my* pleasure." Dylan smiled at all the girls, but DJ sensed that his eyes were on Taylor. Not surprising, since Taylor was his favorite.

"And, just like you asked, I've found a choreographer who has volunteered to donate her time," Grandmother told Dylan. "In fact, some of you girls probably know her—Miss Walford is the dance team coach at Crescent Cove High School." This caused a few of the girls who were dance team members, including Tina and Madison, to clap with enthusiasm.

Grandmother glanced at her watch. "Miss Walford should be here any minute. She had an appointment to attend to first."

"And I brought the music that I'd like you to use." Dylan handed Grandmother a CD.

"Why don't I have the girls do some runs on the catwalk while we wait for Miss Walford to arrive?"

"Sounds like a good plan," Dylan said.

Grandmother clapped her hands, moving over to the stairs by the makeshift runway that they used for practice. "All right, girls, let's get you lined up and ready to go."

"If you don't mind"—Dylan joined Grandmother—"I'd like to arrange them."

"Certainly." Grandmother stepped aside.

"Taylor, you will open the show." He gave her a broad smile. "You'll set the pace for everyone else to follow."

Taylor nodded and went over to stand by him.

Now he scanned the girls. "Daisy, I'd like you to be next. Then DJ, followed by Eliza." Soon he had them lined up. But it seemed clear that he considered the first four to be his starting lineup. And while DJ felt flattered to be in the top four, it also made her a little uneasy. She suspected that some of the others, like Madison and Tina, might be jealous. But at least they couldn't blame anyone but Dylan for this.

"Sorry I'm late," called out Miss Walford as she came into the room. She had on jeans and a sweatshirt — not exactly Grandmother's favorite sort of attire. But Grandmother was gracious to her, introducing her and explaining that they'd already begun to practice.

Soon the music was playing and Miss Walford coached the girls to move in some new ways and to strike some new poses. Dylan pointed out what he liked and what he didn't, then eventually sat down and just watched. This was actually the part about modeling that DJ liked. It felt sort of like a sport and, no different from playing basketball or soccer, DJ focused on doing her best, and that meant imitating Taylor.

"You girls look fantastic," Dylan said when the music ended. "I'm confident that you'll do my styles honor on Mother's Day."

"And everyone is invited downstairs for a light brunch that Clara has prepared for us," Grandmother announced. "Dylan, I hope you can stay a bit before you rush back to the city."

"My pleasure."

Soon they were all down in the dining room, eating and visiting. Madison quickly cornered Dylan, gushing about how much she loved his designs. But DJ wondered if Madison really knew the difference between a Dylan Marceau and a Ralph Lauren. Not that DJ necessarily did. But she didn't pretend to either.

"Do you want to make a break for it?" she asked Taylor as she set down her empty plate.

"Sure." Taylor nodded toward Dylan. "But maybe we should tell him good-bye first."

They went over and thanked Dylan for coming and told him they were leaving, but he wouldn't hear of it. "You girls can't go yet," he said as if he was hurt. "What's so important that you can't spend a little more time with your old buddy Dylan?"

"Just prom dress shopping," DJ admitted.

He nodded. "Well, that is important."

"But we don't have to rush off," Taylor assured him.

He glanced around the room, then back to Taylor. "Is there someplace where we can talk privately?"

"The library," DJ suggested.

"Thank you." Dylan smiled. "And you come too, DJ. I know you and Taylor are good friends."

DJ led the way to the library. She had little doubt about what Dylan was going to say to Taylor. He'd been taken with her right from the beginning. In fact, he'd already made one job offer to her following his New York debut, but Taylor later told him that she needed to finish high school first. And she'd confessed to DJ that she wasn't sure that modeling would be the right fit for her—especially as a new Christian and recovering alcoholic. Taylor grasped that a model's life would come with its challenges.

But as soon as they were seated in the library, Dylan began talking to Taylor about working for him. Following graduation, he wanted her to come to New York. "You would be my top model," he told her. "Both in print and on the runway."

"I'm really flattered," she told him.

"You should be." He grinned. "It's a great opportunity."

"I'm just not sure it's right for me."

"You don't want to model professionally?"

Taylor's face grew thoughtful, but she didn't answer.

"Can I say something?" DJ ventured, glancing at Taylor for affirmation.

"Please, do."

"I think I know why Taylor's hesitant about this," DJ began slowly. "We've all heard about how models get pulled into some pretty crazy lifestyles. My grandmother has shared stories about drugs and alcohol—"

"But not all models fall into that," he said defensively. "Certainly not anyone as grounded and intelligent as Taylor."

"I'm not as grounded as you think," Taylor confessed. Then she proceeded to tell him about her stint in rehab last winter. "I've only been sober for less than four months."

He nodded, taking this in.

"And Taylor's been doing great," DJ assured him. "She hasn't fallen off the wagon once, have you, Taylor?"

"No." Taylor shook her head. "It's too scary to think about because I'm afraid if I fall off, I might not be able to get back on."

Dylan seemed to be considering this.

"So, although your offer is amazing," Taylor continued, "I think it's wiser for me to say no."

"What if DJ came with you?" he said suddenly. "You could both model for me. You two actually look great together, very complementary, and I could use DJ for the more—"

"Wait!" DJ held up her hands. "I don't want to be a model."

He frowned. "You don't?"

"No."

He looked skeptical. "I thought all girls wanted to be models."

"Not DJ," Taylor told him. "She's never been into this. If Mrs. Carter wasn't DJ's grandmother, I'm sure DJ would've never put one foot on the runway. But she's a really good athlete."

He sighed. "So you're turning me down?"

Taylor looked sad as she nodded. And suddenly DJ felt guilty, like it was her fault that Taylor was missing out on this huge opportunity.

"I feel like the spoiler," DJ admitted. "Like if I was willing, Taylor would be—"

"No, don't think that," Taylor said quickly.

"But you are disappointed, aren't you?"

Taylor shrugged.

DJ turned to Dylan. "What if we worked for you during the summer?"

He brightened. "You'd do that?"

DJ nodded. "I could probably use some money for college tuition anyway."

"Yes!" Dylan exclaimed. "You could make some good money in just one summer. I have a good friend with a modeling agency and I'll bet you girls could get some work with her too, if you wanted."

"You're serious?" Taylor asked DJ. "You'd do that for me?"

"Just for one summer," DJ said, wondering if she'd lost her mind completely.

Taylor jumped out of her chair and hugged DJ. "You're the best!"

Dylan was standing now too, shaking both girls' hands. "So, we have a deal then? You girls will come to New York for the summer and work for me?"

DJ felt like she was in shock as Dylan heartily shook her hand. Had she actually agreed to this? Voluntarily? Or was it all just a bad dream?

"You girls have made me the happiest man today," he told them. "In fact, I have an idea. You said you were going prom dress shopping, right?"

DJ nodded glumly. "Not that I was looking forward to it."

"Well, now you don't need to go."

"Huh?"

"I will send both of you original Dylan Marceau gowns."

"Seriously?" Taylor's eyes lit up.

"Yes. We have your measurements and, if you'll trust me, I will design gowns that will look perfect on both of you."

"You're kidding!" DJ could hardly believe her luck. She wasn't going to have to go formal shopping after all.

"I totally trust you," Taylor assured him.

"Me too!"

"To give you a heads-up, my assistant will send you color swatches," he told them.

"Thank you," Taylor said happily.

"Thank *you*," Dylan said back. Then he turned to DJ with real appreciation. "And *thank you*!"

DJ still felt slightly blindsided as they rejoined the others. She couldn't believe what she'd just agreed to, and even wondered if it still might be possible to back out of it. She'd apologize to Dylan and Taylor, explaining that she'd simply suffered temporary insanity. Then, before she knew what was happening, Dylan was telling Grandmother about their little agreement.

"Oh, Dylan," Grandmother gushed. "That is fabulous! Absolutely fabulous!" She reached for DJ, pulling her close. "Oh, Desiree, you have made me so happy and proud!"

"But I —"

"Listen, listen, everyone," Grandmother was calling out now. "We have an announcement to make—the most wonderful news! Dylan, you tell them!"

And suddenly Dylan was standing there in the dining room explaining to everyone how he'd just hired Taylor and DJ to model for him following graduation. Feeling slightly sick to her stomach, DJ watched the girls' faces as they reacted to this "wonderful news." Some, like Casey and Rhiannon, looked just as stunned as DJ felt. Others, like Madison and Tina and maybe even Eliza, looked seriously envious.

What in the world had DJ gotten herself into? And was it too late to get out?

**"I'm so proud of you, dear."** Grandmother's eyes lit up as she patted DJ's cheek with affection. DJ, Taylor, and Rhiannon had just gotten home from church when Grandmother stopped DJ in the foyer. "It's so wonderful that you and Taylor have been selected to model for Dylan. Such a marvelous opportunity. I've already contacted a real-estate friend in Manhattan to find you girls a small studio to share. You must be so excited!"

DJ forced a smile. "I guess. Just don't forget that I'll only be doing this for the summer—just to earn some money for college."

Grandmother smiled knowingly. "Yes, yes ... we'll see, won't we."

DJ knew better than to argue. Grandmother had already told DJ in no uncertain terms that "any girl with any sense" would model for as long as she could and attend college later. "You're in your prime now," she had insisted. "Trust me, it will end quickly enough." As if DJ were some kind of hothouse orchid that would soon wilt and be worthless. DJ decided it was best to simply humor her. Besides, it was rather nice to be in Grandmother's good graces for a change.

Fortunately, the general arrived in time to cut Grandmother's little praise-fest short. "You two have a nice lunch," DJ called as they left. Then she turned to see Casey at the top of the stairs, just standing there as if she'd been listening.

"Hey, Case," DJ called out cheerfully as she hurried to catch her. "What's up?"

Casey frowned. "Nothing."

"What's wrong?"

"What makes you think something's wrong?"

"Your face." DJ winced at how that probably sounded. "I mean you look unhappy."

"Unhappy compared to what?"

"Huh?"

"I mean, just because your life's all sweetness and light doesn't mean that everyone else is miserable."

"No, of course not. And, just for the record, my life *isn't* all sweetness and light."

"Yeah, right."

"If you're talking about the modeling gig, trust me, it's not anything I wanted."

Casey's eyes narrowed. "Then why are you doing it?"

DJ glanced over to her closed bedroom door. Not that she would say anything that Taylor didn't already know.

"I know why you're doing it," Casey continued. "Because you think you're helping Taylor. But you know what I think?"

"What?"

"I think you're doing it to help yourself."

DJ shrugged. "Well, it'll be nice to earn some college money."

"I'm sure that's part of why you're doing it. But I think, even though you complain about all this fashion biz, you secretly like it."

DJ laughed. "That's nuts."

"I don't think so, DJ. I've known you for a long time, and you've always been out there doing sports, soaking up all the glory—you love being the center of attention."

"I do not."

Casey nodded. "I think you do."

DJ didn't know what to say. And what was the point of this conversation anyway? Why was Casey needling her like this? "So, what if you're right, Casey? Suppose I do like the limelight? What difference does that make to you?"

Casey seemed to consider this. "It just proves to me that you really have changed."

"But you said I was *always* like that . . . that I *always* wanted to be the center of attention."

"Well, you're just not who I thought you were, DJ. That's all I'm saying."

DJ had to control herself. She wanted to shoot the exact same accusation back at Casey, but knew that would probably start a fight. And DJ did not want to fight. "I guess we all change . . ." she said quietly. "I mean, it's probably just part of growing up. No one can stay the same."

Casey nodded sadly. "Yeah, I guess you're right."

"Hey, Casey," called Rhiannon, "I thought you were coming to look at my sketches for your dress."

"Yeah, I'm coming." Casey turned and followed Rhiannon into her room. And DJ just stood there scratching her head. What was that conversation really about? And why did it feel like Casey was mad at her?

Eliza emerged from her room looking exasperated. "I really think that Casey and Rhiannon should go back to being roommates. It's like the little dressmaker is taking over all the space in there."

DJ tried not to laugh, since everyone knew that Eliza normally hogged not only the closets but most of the room as well. "Maybe you can talk Kriti into switching with her."

"Maybe." Eliza frowned. "Speaking of Kriti, did she remind you that my campaign party is tonight at six?"

"Yes, and I can hardly wait."

Eliza put her face close to DJ's. "Just because you and Taylor think you're about to become supermodels doesn't mean you have to treat the rest of us like dirt."

"I'm not treating anyone like dirt."

"Well, just in case this whole New York modeling thing goes to your head ..."

DJ rolled her eyes. "Yeah, right."

"And, FYI, I know the real reason Dylan asked you."

"Huh?"

Eliza gave her a knowing look as she lowered her voice. "It's so you can make sure Taylor doesn't mess up. You're kind of like a really expensive babysitter."

"Think what you like." DJ turned to go to her room.

"See you at six," Eliza called in a sugary voice.

DJ went into her room and let out a loud sigh.

"What's wrong?" Taylor looked up from where she was working on her laptop.

"Just your average green-eyed monster."

"Let me guess ..." Taylor laid her forefinger alongside her face. "Eliza is jerking your chain about Dylan."

"Bingo."

"Well, what did you expect?"

DJ sunk down onto her bed. "I don't know ... I just hope it blows over soon."

"Were you paying attention to the sermon this morning?"

DJ thought about church. "For the most part." Then she paused. "Although I suppose I did space out a little." The truth

38

was she'd still been fretting over her agreement with Dylan Marceau, wishing there was an easy way out.

"Remember the part about welcoming your trials as friends?"

DJ nodded. "Or in our case ... we welcome our friends as trials?"

Taylor laughed. "I guess that works."

"So I need to remember that the hard stuff, like Eliza's jabs or Casey's criticism, might actually be God's way of making me stronger." DJ flopped onto her back to think about this. "Kind of like training for sports—it's not easy to build muscles and get into shape."

"No pain, no gain."

"That's true." DJ closed her eyes and took in a deep breath, then slowly let it out. "Oh, by the way, don't forget Eliza's prom queen campaign party at six."

Taylor groaned. "Thanks for reminding me."

"No pain, no gain." And DJ knew that Eliza's campaign party, despite her promise of food, would be painful. At least for DJ since she did not get why something so silly should matter so much. Seriously, why was Eliza so driven to win a silly crown that would be forgotten in a few days? What did it really matter? And although Eliza had always been competitive—whether to prove something to herself or her friends or even her parents—it seemed like it had intensified recently. DJ wasn't sure what was behind Eliza's obsession, but it was fierce.

And though it made no sense, DJ wondered if Eliza's need to reign over the prom was related to what had happened to her in Palm Beach. Not that anyone was allowed to bring up that particular subject. Grandmother had made that perfectly clear after they'd returned to Crescent Cove. The Carter House girls and their boyfriends were expected to respect Eliza's privacy—

and that meant not discussing or repeating the Palm Beach incident to anyone. Grandmother had even gone so far as to enlist the general to do everything possible to keep the whole thing under wraps both in Florida and at home. Although rumors had circulated in school for a few days, some kids had actually believed the whole thing was a hoax. And it soon blew over. Or so it seemed. DJ wasn't sure. Maybe Eliza hoped that a crown on her head would erase the humiliation of being kidnapped by a jerk who had pretended to be a boyfriend. DJ didn't think that was possible.

"I want to thank you all for coming tonight." Eliza stood up by the fireplace, dressed immaculately in a pale yellow blouse and white pants. Every golden hair was in place as she struck an "elegant" pose, almost as if she thought the photographers would arrive any moment and start snapping publicity shots. She smiled as she looked out over her "captive" audience of the other five Carter House girls plus Daisy and Ariel, friends from modeling class. "I so appreciate your help in my campaign. As you know, Daisy is my campaign manager. I invited her to speak tonight, but she insisted I should do it."

Daisy giggled. "I'm lousy at speeches."

"That's okay," Eliza assured her in a placating tone. "We all have our different gifts."

DJ leaned back into the couch and tried to stay awake as Eliza droned on about how critical the next two weeks would be in winning the crown for her. She sounded so serious, so sincere … it was like she thought this was a presidential campaign. "I expect you all to wear buttons and … I have a little surprise." She reached down to the pink canvas bag on the table beside her. "Kriti had T-shirts made up for everyone." She shook out a pink T-shirt with Eliza's face printed on the front, complete with a rhinestone-encrusted crown as well as the words *Queen Eliza* printed beneath. "Aren't these spectacular!" She beamed at Kriti. "Great job!"

"My uncle has a silk screen shop," Kriti said almost apologetically.

"I expect you all to wear these," Eliza told them. "And give them to anyone who promises to be a supporter. But keep in mind, we only ordered a hundred." She reached into her bag of tricks again. "And to sweeten the deal"—she held up a small pink box with graphics similar to the T-shirt—"chocolate." Between the T-shirts, buttons, chocolates, posters, and other junk, DJ estimated this campaign must've cost a bundle. Not that Eliza had reason to be concerned about that. But DJ thought it was a waste. Plus she felt sorry for Haley, who was campaigning on a shoestring. DJ wouldn't make a big deal of it, but she planned to vote for Haley. And if it weren't for Grandmother's pressure and DJ's desire to keep the peace (plus the fact there was food involved), DJ wouldn't be sitting here right now. Eliza was in for a surprise if she honestly thought DJ was going to wear that stupid T-shirt. In her dreams—although DJ knew she wouldn't even wear something like that to bed!

"So, let's go ahead and enjoy dinner, which I'm sure must be set up by now." Eliza glanced at her watch. "Then we'll reconvene on the third floor to make some new posters and put together goodie bags for the voters." She clapped her hands. "And just wait until you see the cool stuff we've got for the goodie bags!"

DJ forced a congenial smile as she filled her plate. The dinner was buffet style, catered by the local Thai restaurant, and it actually looked delicious. DJ finally dropped a couple of prawns on top of the rest of her food, then went and sat at the game table in a quiet corner of the living room—hoping this would keep her far away from Eliza. But Eliza seemed to have other plans because she came over and sat right next to DJ.

"You're running a very slick campaign," DJ told her.

"Thank you." Eliza nodded as if that were a great compliment.

Then, to DJ's relief, Taylor came over. "Nice food, Eliza," she said as she sat down across from DJ and opened her chopsticks.

"Thank you. I hope everyone appreciates it."

"You've really put a lot of money into your campaign." DJ picked up a prawn and studied Eliza's expression.

"You know what they say." Eliza smiled.

"What?"

She held up her hands. "It's only money."

"Oh . . ."

"But is it really worth it?" Taylor ventured.

Eliza stiffened. "What do you mean?"

"I mean is it worth all this just to be elected prom queen?"

Eliza glared at Taylor. "Well . . . it is to me."

"I didn't mean to offend you," Taylor said sincerely. "I just wondered."

"I have to admit that I wondered too," DJ said. "I mean, it's like you're taking it so seriously."

Eliza leaned toward them. "The truth is . . . I am very serious about it. I really, really want this. I know you both probably think I'm shallow and silly, but I really want to be prom queen. You can make fun of me. In fact, I'm sure you already do." She looked close to tears now. "But this is really important to me. And I'd . . . I'd just appreciate it if you two—*especially you two*— would support me in this. It's not like I've ever won anything before. DJ, you won homecoming queen. And Taylor's going to be Dylan Marceau's next hot model. I just want to finally win something. Is that so bad?"

DJ was speechless and it seemed Taylor was too.

"Is that too much to ask?" Eliza demanded.

"No," Taylor said quickly. "It's not too much. And I really appreciate your honesty, Eliza. I'll support you in this."

"Me too," DJ agreed. "I didn't feel that supportive before ... but hearing how much it means to you ... well, I'll do what I can to help."

Eliza looked immensely relieved. "Thank you."

"But I have to draw the line," DJ said hesitantly.

"Where?" Eliza looked suspicious.

"I won't wear that T-shirt. I'm sorry, but I just won't."

Eliza looked slightly offended, but then nodded. "Okay."

Just then Daisy called to Eliza from across the room.

"Will you please excuse me?" Eliza said politely.

"Certainly." Taylor nodded. As soon as Eliza was out of earshot she whispered, "I totally agree about the T-shirt, DJ. I just didn't want to rock Eliza's boat more than necessary."

DJ chuckled. "Poor Eliza. She *really* wants to be prom queen."

"Who knew?"

"I had actually been secretly planning to defect to Haley's campaign ... but I guess I won't now."

"Well, I meant what I said. It won't be easy, but I will campaign for her."

"Yeah, me too."

Later on, when they were all up in the ballroom, DJ and Taylor both worked wholeheartedly on a poster together. And the end results weren't bad.

"That's beautiful!" Eliza told them. "I love it!"

"Thanks." DJ stood up to look at it. Okay, it was a little too pink and glitzy for her taste, but it did look professional.

"Hey, I meant to ask you guys," Eliza said. "Did you get your prom dresses yesterday?"

Taylor glanced uneasily at DJ.

"You didn't go shopping?" Eliza's tone had an accusing edge to it. "What is wrong with you two?"

"Actually, it's taken care of," Taylor assured her.

"Taken care of?"

DJ screwed the top back onto the glitter jar. "Yes, no need to worry. It's all under control."

"How is that possible?" Eliza placed her hands on her hips. "Please, tell me you're not ordering them online. You know how bad that could be."

"No, nothing like that," Taylor said quickly.

"Come on, you guys, just tell me," she pleaded. "I can't stand the suspense."

Taylor looked at DJ and DJ just shrugged.

"Well, it's not like it's some state secret," Taylor said. "Dylan offered to help us with our dresses."

"Dylan Marceau is designing your prom dresses?" Of course, she said this so loudly that everyone else in the room heard it.

"Yeah, it's not that big of a deal," DJ told her.

"Original Marceau gowns aren't a big deal?"

"You have a designer gown too," DJ pointed out.

Eliza nodded. "Yes ... but I plan to be prom queen. I need a special gown."

Taylor laughed. "So the rest of us should go slumming just to make you look better?"

Eliza glanced to see if everyone was watching her now. "No, of course not. Everyone should look their best." She made what looked like a forced smile. "I think it's lovely that all three of us will be wearing designer gowns."

But as the other girls looked on, curiously studying Taylor and DJ and Eliza, it suddenly felt like the three of them were in some kind of snooty elitist club. And DJ wished she knew the secret handshake to get herself kicked out.

"TIME FOR A NEW SHOW OF HANDS," Harry announced to their lunch table on Monday. He did this a couple of times a week, and DJ was getting a little tired of it. "Who still hasn't received their college admissions letter?"

Several sheepishly stuck up their hands.

"Hey, your hand's not up," Harry said to Lane.

Lane made a poker face like he usually did. He'd been wait-listed since February and was not very pleased about it. "My letter from Yale finally came."

"And?" Harry waited.

"Accepted." Lane grinned as they exchanged a high five.

"Congrats, man," said Harry. "Just too bad you had to settle for Yale."

Lane laughed. "That's what I'd expect from someone who couldn't strive for anything better than Princeton."

Then, as usual, the argument over which Ivy League school was superior began to broil.

Even Kriti got involved, claiming that Harry and Lane were both wrong. "Harvard beats them both out." She punched Josh in the arm. "Right?"

"Absolutely," he said with good humor. "Everybody knows that Harvard rocks."

"Come on," Lane urged Eliza, "you're a Yale girl. Help me defend our school."

"Wait a minute," Harry corrected him. "Eliza hasn't been accepted at Yale yet, has she?"

Eliza looked slightly embarrassed. She too had been wait-listed, although she'd been boasting that it was just a matter of time. "So, when did you say your letter came, Lane?"

"Saturday."

Her mouth twisted. "Well, mine might've been sent to Louisville."

"Have you called home to see?"

She shrugged. "They'll let me know." Then she turned to DJ. "Hey, you applied to Yale too. Have you heard anything?"

DJ rolled her eyes. "No, and I'm not holding my breath. I only did it for Grandmother's sake, plus I was a late applicant so I don't expect to hear anytime soon." She glanced at Conner, then grinned. "Besides, I already got accepted to Wesleyan U. And they even offered a small athletic scholarship package."

Lane waved his hand dismissively. "Well, that figures. They have to bribe students to come to *that* tiny school."

Conner frowned, but didn't engage. His parents were Wesleyan U alumni and he'd been sold on the small Middletown university for years. To be honest, Conner was the main reason that DJ had even considered this school in the first place. But after some investigation, DJ thought a small college would be perfect for someone like her. To her relief, the bell rang and the disagreement ended.

As DJ headed for class, she tried not to feel irked at her friends' "lighthearted banter," as Harry called it. Still, it bugged her. Why couldn't they discuss something without turning it into a major competition? Not that she didn't like competition when it came to sports, where the rules were clear-cut and the victory was the result of skill and hard work, but when people fought over subjective things like fashion or colleges or even prom queen . . . well, it seemed a little crazy.

DJ was just rounding the corner toward the Social Studies department when she noticed Casey emerging from the restroom. Her face was flushed and it looked like she'd been crying. DJ realized that both Casey and Seth had been absent from the lunch table.

"Case?" DJ approached her with hesitation. "You okay?"

"Fine," Casey snapped.

"What's wrong?"

"Nothing."

"But—"

"I'm late for class." Then Casey took off in the other direction.

DJ's best guess was that Casey and Seth had gotten into a fight. And she actually hoped that was the case. In fact, DJ wouldn't feel the least bit disappointed if they broke up completely. Oh, Casey would pout for a while, but in the long run, it would be for the best. DJ shot up a silent prayer for Casey as she took her seat in history. And she continued to pray for her off and on throughout the day.

After school was out and she was driving Taylor and Rhiannon home, DJ queried whether they'd seen Casey that afternoon.

"Why?" Taylor probed. "Is something wrong?"

"Maybe."

"What happened?" Rhiannon asked.

"She'd been crying. And when I tried to talk with her, she blew me off. But it was obvious she was upset."

"Do you think something happened with Seth?" Taylor asked.

"That's my guess." DJ sighed. "I just wish she'd talk to me."

"She's been shutting me down too," Rhiannon admitted. "Especially if I say one word that sounds negative about Seth."

"And she won't even give me the time of day," Taylor told them. "But that's nothing new."

"Probably because you know more about Seth than most people," DJ said as she turned into the Carter House driveway to drop them off.

"Aren't you getting out?" Taylor asked as she reached for her bag.

"No, I need to run to the bank and then to the Mockingbird Gallery."

"Oh, yeah," Rhiannon said. "The painting."

"Yeah. I'll see you later. Don't mention it to my grandmother, okay?" DJ had already told them it was meant to be a Mother's Day surprise.

They waved, and DJ drove back to town. She quickly took care of the banking business, then went and purchased the painting. She was just heading back toward home when she noticed Casey walking by herself on a side street. Whispering another quick prayer, DJ slowly pulled up alongside Casey, rolled down the window, and asked her if she wanted to get some coffee.

Casey simply shrugged and continued walking.

"Come on," DJ urged. "My treat."

"Are you going to stalk me if I don't?"

DJ laughed. "Yeah, I think so."

Casey got into the car, and DJ drove them over to McHenry's. While Casey sat down at a table in a quiet corner, DJ ordered them both a mocha with extra whipped cream. She silently prayed as she carried the drinks to the table. *Please, God, help me to say the right words. Don't let this turn into a fight. Please!*

"Here you go." She set the mocha in front of Casey. "Just the way you like it. At least the way you used to like it."

Casey barely nodded, and her eyes remained on the coffee. "Yeah ... some things don't change."

DJ sat down and took in a slow breath. "Casey, I know that I'm a great one for putting my foot in my mouth. And I'm sure I've done all kinds of things to offend you. But I'm really sorry, okay? I still really love you. And I wish you still thought of me as your friend."

Casey was still looking down, but her chin was trembling. She reached for a napkin and blotted her cheeks.

"See, I did it again, didn't I?" DJ shook her head. "I guess I should just keep my mouth shut, huh?"

Casey didn't respond. She just continued to look down, occasionally blotting the tears that kept streaming down her face.

Meanwhile, DJ prayed. She didn't know what else to do.

Finally, after what felt like an hour, Casey looked up with watery eyes. "It's not your fault, DJ," she said in a husky voice.

"Do you want to talk?"

Casey let out a ragged sigh, then nodded, but she didn't say a word.

"Does it have to do with Seth?"

She nodded again.

"Did you guys break up?"

"Not yet."

"Oh ..."

"But it's probably just a matter of time."

"Is it mutual?"

51

Casey bit her lip, then shook her head no.

DJ's patience was wearing thin. She didn't want to play Twenty Questions. On the other hand, she didn't want to alienate Casey either. Not when it seemed like she really needed a friend.

"I told Seth something today . . ." Casey's voice was so quiet, DJ could barely hear her. "Something he didn't want to hear."

DJ felt a flutter of hope. Maybe Casey was the one who wanted to break up. Maybe that had made Seth mad. "And?"

"And he was furious. Totally unreasonable."

"Uh-huh?" DJ nodded like she was following this.

"It's such a mess, DJ. I don't know what to do."

"I'd like to help you, Casey, really I would. But you're going to have to tell me more. Was Seth mad because you tried to break up?"

"No." She shook her head. "That's not it."

A jolt of panic hit DJ. "Casey," she said, "is it . . . are you . . . Remember what you told me in Palm Beach? Are you pregnant?"

Casey looked down again. But DJ knew she was right. And as unreasonable as it was, DJ felt mad. Why had Casey allowed herself to get into this place? Why had she been so stupid? And why had she pushed everyone away? And what was she going to do now? All these questions made DJ's head hurt.

"I tried to believe that I wasn't pregnant," Casey admitted. "I guess I was kind of in denial. But it just seemed so impossible. I really convinced myself that I wasn't."

"Do you know for sure that you are?"

"I did a home pregnancy test this weekend. I did it three times just to be sure." She blew her nose on the napkin. "Two pink stripes each time."

DJ blinked. "Two pink stripes?"

"On the test strips . . . it means I'm pregnant."

"Oh ... Casey ..." DJ reached across the table and put her hand over Casey's. "That's got to be so hard."

She nodded and sniffed. "And when I told Seth ... well, he hasn't been sympathetic. He acts like it's all my fault."

"Your fault? Like you *wanted* to get pregnant?" DJ tried to keep her voice calm. "What about Seth? Shouldn't he take some responsibility?"

Casey didn't answer.

"I mean, you told me about this in Palm Beach ... about how he pressured you ... and how he didn't even use anything—"

"That wasn't the only time we had sex."

DJ wasn't sure how to respond. She wasn't even sure how much she wanted to hear. And yet she knew Casey needed to talk—needed a friend. And so DJ just nodded and pretended to understand, when all she really wanted to do was to shake Casey and say things like, "I told you so." Thankfully, she didn't.

"Anyway, Seth says it's my fault, and that it's up to the girl to keep this from happening, and—"

"That's ridiculous, Casey. It obviously takes two people to make a baby. How can you go around blaming just one?"

"But Seth said I should've been using birth control."

DJ took in a slow breath. "So ... are you saying you guys never used *anything*?"

Casey looked down. "Not exactly ..." she mumbled.

"Oh." DJ didn't know what to say. Really, all this was so outside of her comfort zone. She could hardly believe they were sitting in McHenry's talking about having sex and being pregnant. What happened to the days when they would sit here and talk about soccer or the latest movie?

"We'd been drinking," Casey admitted. "I know it was stupid. And I just didn't realize it was going to go that far."

DJ wanted to point out that Casey, under the influence, wasn't terribly sensible. But she didn't want to shut her down.

"Later on we used protection." Casey wadded her tear-soaked napkin into a tight little ball and picked up a fresh one. "Obviously, it was too late."

"So how far along do you think you are?"

"My best guess is that it happened the night of the Rockabilly dance."

DJ pressed her lips together tightly. She was *not* going to say anything that remotely sounded like "I told you so."

"I know what you're thinking, DJ."

She looked evenly at Casey. "What?"

"That I'm an idiot."

"No." DJ firmly shook her head. "You're not an idiot. But you are in a tough spot, Case. What do you plan to do?"

Casey blotted fresh tears. "I—I don't know. Seth wants me to get an abortion. In fact, he's insisting I get an abortion."

"Insisting?" DJ felt indignant. How dare he?

"Yeah, he says it's the only option. He wants to pay for it. And he told me not to tell anyone that I'm pregnant either."

"Have you told anyone?"

"Just you. Even then I tried to take it back."

"Yeah . . . I know."

"Seth really doesn't want anyone to know, DJ. His parents will freak if they find out."

"What about *your* parents?"

"They'll freak too." She locked eyes with DJ. "You're the only one besides Seth and me that knows. You have to promise me you won't tell anyone."

DJ just nodded.

"You swear?"

"Of course. It's your secret, Casey. And, if it makes you feel any better, I never told anyone what you told me in Palm Beach either."

"I know. I could tell."

"And it's not easy." DJ looked down at her barely touched mocha. "Especially when you're acting all weird and pushing everyone away from you like we're the enemy."

"It was just easier that way. I was afraid that if I actually talked to you — or even Rhiannon — I might spill the beans." She held up her hands in ,a hopeless gesture. "Like I just did."

"It must be lonely ... keeping all that to yourself."

"You have no idea."

"But you shouldn't isolate yourself, Casey. Don't forget, you have friends. I'm your friend. You know that, don't you?"

"I know."

"And you can't do this alone."

Casey sat up straighter now. "But, besides you, DJ, I don't want anyone to know. Don't forget you promised."

"But shouldn't you see a doctor?"

"Why?"

DJ shrugged. "I don't know. It just seems like the normal thing to — "

"Nothing about this feels normal to me."

"Yeah ... but ..."

"I'm just not ready for that yet." Her jaw grew firm, and DJ could hear the warning in her voice.

"Okay ..." DJ took a sip of her lukewarm mocha.

Casey's expression softened. "But I do appreciate your friendship. And I appreciate you keeping this quiet."

"Can I ask you a question?"

"Sure ... what?"

"How do you feel?"

Casey wrapped her hands around her coffee cup and creased her brow. "I don't know ... I mean, besides depressed and confused and slightly suicidal—"

"Suicidal?" DJ gasped.

"Maybe that's an overstatement."

"But you are depressed?"

"Wouldn't you be if you were in my shoes?"

DJ wanted to say that she would never be in Casey's shoes, but knew that was heartless. "Actually, when I asked how you felt, I didn't mean emotionally exactly ... I meant how do you feel about ... about ... the baby?"

Casey took a long, slow sip of mocha, then set the cup down and looked directly at DJ. "Right now, it's hard to believe there's really a baby inside of me. I mean, my body definitely feels different and I have no doubt that I'm pregnant. But I just can't grasp that a living human being is inside of me. And Seth keeps telling me that there's only *fetal matter*." She scowled. "And that infuriates me."

"It probably just makes it easier for him—you know, to tell you to get an abortion."

"I know. But do you remember how I used to help my mom on her pro-life campaigns?"

DJ did remember, vividly. "I even helped you guys one summer."

"Remember those posters of unborn babies?"

"Yeah ... the little fingers and toes."

"So I'm not stupid ... I know it's not 'fetal matter.' "

DJ just nodded.

"I may be confused about a lot of things, but I still feel that abortion is murder."

"So you're not going to do it?"

Casey looked down at her mocha again.

"Case?"

"I don't know. I mean, even though it's wrong, it's really tempting. According to my parents, I've already done something wrong—really wrong. What difference does it make if I do something else wrong?"

"Two wrongs don't make a right."

Casey rolled her eyes. "Thanks for that brilliant advice."

"Sorry, but I think your parents would agree."

"But think about it, DJ. Which would make my parents happier—if I came home after graduation and announced that I was knocked up or if I didn't?"

"But if they knew?"

"What if they didn't?"

DJ sensed that they were close to a real argument now, and she didn't see how that could help anything. So she reached over and put her hand on Casey's again. "Whatever happens, Case, just remember that I'm here for you. Okay?"

"Thanks." Casey stifled a yawn. "Now if you don't mind, could we go home? Something about being pregnant makes me sleepier than usual. I'd like to catch a nap before dinner."

"No problem."

DJ felt conflicted as she drove them home. On one hand, she was thankful that Casey had finally been honest with her. On the other hand, ignorance had been pretty blissful.

**6**

*Last Dance*

**FOR THE NEXT FEW DAYS,** Casey kept a low profile both at school and at home. But at least she had stopped picking fights with everyone. Still, DJ felt uneasy about the situation; it was kind of like Casey was a kettle left sitting on the stove — just simmering for the time being but ready to boil over at any given moment. DJ had initiated a couple of guarded conversations, but Casey had been careful to avoid anything remotely linked to her pregnancy or how she planned to deal with it. Consequently, DJ felt like she was sitting on a huge and potentially volatile secret. And she would've been much more comfortable just getting it out in the open. Yet, that wasn't for her to do.

"Casey seems happier," Taylor said to DJ as they got ready for school on Thursday. "She was actually pretty congenial at youth group last night. I was afraid we were going to have to bind and gag and drag her in."

"I think she's trying to honor her word with Rhiannon."

"And it seems like she's not mad at you anymore." Taylor studied DJ as they both stood in front of the large bathroom mirror. "Did you guys have a little chat or something?"

"Sort of."

"And did she tell you why she'd been mad?"

"Not exactly ... but we buried the hatchet anyway. I told Casey that she needs friends and it's crazy for her to push us all away."

"That's for sure. Anyone with Seth for a boyfriend really does need friends. Too bad she didn't break up like we thought."

DJ nodded. "Yeah, it is too bad."

"Not that we're going to say as much to her."

"No way." DJ wanted to warn Taylor that the best way to handle Casey these days was with great care, but she knew that would only raise questions.

Once they were at the breakfast table, it seemed obvious that Grandmother had an announcement to make. DJ could always tell by the way Grandmother sat erect and straight, watching and waiting with bright eyes as the girls all sat down. And, sure enough, she was now ringing her water glass with a butter knife. "I have some happy news," she told them. "I would've shared it last night at dinnertime, but some of you girls were gone to your youth group." She then held up an envelope with a crest on it. It appeared to have already been opened. "We have heard from Yale."

DJ squinted to see the front of the envelope, but Grandmother was already opening it and reading what turned out to be an acceptance letter. And it was for DJ. She had not only been accepted as an incoming student to Yale, but she'd been invited to visit the campus to meet with the athletic director. Still, it irked her that Grandmother had opened the letter first. Weren't there laws against reading someone else's mail? And to do it in public! DJ looked down at her clenched fists in her lap, then realized that she needed to let this go. Grandmother was, after all, Grandmother.

"Congratulations," Taylor told her.

"That's great, DJ," Rhiannon added.

"Way to go," Casey said with a tiny spark of enthusiasm.

Even Kriti, the Harvard-bound girl, seemed to be glad for DJ. But Eliza remained silent.

"I'm very pleased for you, DJ," Grandmother gushed. "I hope you know what an honor this is. Yale is a very distinguished school. And I know your great-grandfather would be very proud."

"I'm totally stunned," DJ admitted. And that was true. Her SAT scores were good, and her grades were solid, but not stellar. She'd applied only to appease her grandmother. She never dreamed they'd accept her. How was that even possible? And what would she do now?

"I'm stunned too," Eliza said quietly. "Especially considering that DJ applied so late in the game. So ... when did that letter come, Mrs. Carter?"

Grandmother considered this. "Well, I hadn't gone through the mail for a couple of days ... but I'm sure it arrived this week. Perhaps Monday or Tuesday. Why, dear?"

"Please excuse me." Eliza was already out of her chair and opening her cell phone with a look of determination. DJ's guess was that she was calling home to see if a letter had come for her as well. Hopefully it had.

"So, DJ ..." Kriti's dark eyes were curious. "Does this mean you'll cut your modeling career short?"

DJ glanced at Taylor, then at Grandmother. "I only committed to work for Dylan throughout the summer. I'd always planned to go to college."

Kriti smiled in approval. "Good for you."

"I'm so proud of all you girls," Grandmother said happily. "I'm sure you all have bright futures ahead." She turned to Rhiannon.

"And I expect we should be hearing from the Fashion Institute of Technology soon. If you'd like, I could check on it for you."

"Oh, would you?"

"I'd be glad to. In fact, I'll let them know that you've been accepted at NYU. Maybe that'll help them to see that they don't want to lose you."

"Thank you, Mrs. Carter."

Eliza never returned to the breakfast table. DJ wasn't sure if that meant good news or bad. Out of curiosity, she looked around the house for Eliza, but by the time she found her, Eliza and Kriti were already rushing out the front door and hurrying out to her car. Eliza's expression was unreadable.

At lunchtime, Taylor needled Harry to do the college acceptance hand count again. And when it was revealed that DJ had been accepted at Yale, Lane gave out a loud whoop. Then he dashed around the table and swooped her up into a hug and happy dance.

"But I'm not sure I'm even going." She glanced quickly at Conner, giving him a helpless look, but he just smiled in a patient way.

"Why not?" Lane demanded.

"Because it's *not* Princeton," Harry called out.

"Or Harvard," teased Josh.

"Hey, how about you?" Lane turned to Eliza. "If DJ and I got our letters, you must've gotten yours too."

Eliza frowned at Lane, then sort of glared at DJ, but she said nothing.

"Come on, what did you hear?"

Thankfully, Lane's attention was diverted to Eliza now. DJ used the opportunity to go sit next to Conner.

"Congrats," he said quietly and in a way that didn't sound genuinely happy.

"Come on, Eliza," Lane pestered. "Out with it. You got a letter, didn't you? Or was it an email notification? They're doing that too. I hear the reject note is pretty heartless."

She just tipped her nose up ever so slightly. "I'm not even sure I *want* to go to Yale."

"You were rejected!" Harry pointed his finger at her. "I can see it in your eyes."

"My father said that we don't know that for absolute sure yet." Eliza was reaching for her purse now, looking like she was about to make a fast break.

"Meaning Daddy's going to buy you a nice building to make sure you get in?" Harry gave her a coy look.

"You should know," she shot back at him. "Didn't your family give Princeton a gymnasium or something?"

He laughed. "Not quite."

"But back to DJ." Lane pointed at her. "I want to know why you'd turn down Yale."

"Probably because she'd rather model in New York," Eliza suggested.

"No way!" DJ shook her head. "I would not choose modeling over college."

"Then why not?" demanded Lane.

DJ glanced at Conner, who was still remaining pretty quiet. "Because I think I'd rather go to Wesleyan U."

Of course, this got them all arguing again about which school was best. DJ glanced at Conner and gave her head a nod toward the door, and he got the hint. Soon they were outside.

Conner's eyes looked concerned. "I hope you don't go with Wesleyan U just because of me, DJ. It's pretty small potatoes compared to Yale."

She laughed. "Of course you're not the reason I'd go there. I mean, I really like you Conner, but you're not going to tell me where to go to school."

He sighed. "You know I want you to be there, but I'd feel guilty if you gave up Yale for my sake and regretted it later."

"I'm just not the Yale type, Conner. You know that."

He grinned. "That's a relief. Seriously, I'm not sure that I'm up to competing with those Yale dudes."

She grabbed his hand and squeezed it. "Don't worry, you won't have to. It's flattering that Yale accepted me, but I can't help thinking it was actually a mistake. Besides, you know what I think about Wesleyan. I was totally impressed when I checked them out. I love the small personal feeling of the campus. I was also impressed with how quickly they got back to me. And it's pretty cool that they're offering me a little bit of an athletic scholarship."

"You're a good athlete, DJ—why wouldn't they offer you something?"

"Well, I appreciated it. And I'm pretty sure that's where I'm going."

"Pretty sure, but not positive?"

"Well … I'm pretty positive that I don't want to go to Yale."

"What about your grandmother? Won't she be set on having you go there?"

DJ let out a loud breath. "Maybe it's time I quit letting other people tell me what to do."

He held up his hands defensively. "Not me!"

"No, I didn't mean you, Conner. You seem to be the only one who doesn't try to influence me like that. I mean, first I cave to do the modeling thing, but that's more because of Taylor than Grandmother. Although I'll admit that it's a way to make some good money for college … but still. Then I cave to Eliza to help with her silly prom queen campaign. Which reminds me, I was supposed to take a shift at her campaign table after school today." She groaned. "Just shoot me."

Conner laughed. "Maybe you're just being a good friend."

"I wonder if it's possible to be too good of a friend." Now DJ considered Casey's situation and how she'd bound DJ to silence … and how badly DJ wanted to tell someone, if only to ask for advice. But how could she?

"Well, you've got a good head on your shoulders, DJ. And I know you pray about all this stuff. I'm sure you'll figure it out."

"So …" DJ paused as they were walking across the courtyard and looked into his face. "Are you really glad that I'll be at school with you next year, Conner?"

He grinned. "Of course! But I do feel a little selfish about it. I hate to admit it, but getting accepted to Yale is a big deal. Do you think you should look into it a little? Did they offer any scholarships?"

"They invited me to come visit … and to meet with their athletic director." DJ felt a little flaky now. Why couldn't she just make up her mind?

He looked slightly impressed, or maybe he was just trying to act that way. "That sounds positive."

"I guess it wouldn't hurt to visit," she ventured, "and it would make Grandmother happy to know that I didn't just brush them off without any consideration. Then I could come home and tell her that it just didn't feel like the right fit for me."

"Unless it was the right fit." Conner's expression was serious now.

She firmly shook her head. "Seriously, Conner, you know me. I'm not the Ivy League type."

He gave her a hug. "I think you could do just about anything you set your mind to do, DJ."

"Thanks. I appreciate that vote of confidence. But maybe I better figure out what I want to set my mind to first."

"Casey's sick," Rhiannon told DJ after breakfast on Saturday morning. "She wants you."

"Okay." DJ set down her toothbrush. "Where is she?"

"Locked in our bathroom," Rhiannon said. "Hurry."

DJ tossed an I-don't-know glance to Taylor, then hurried over to Casey's room and quietly knocked on the bathroom door. "It's me, Case, do you want to let me in?"

The door opened and DJ slipped in and closed it in time to see Casey doubling over the toilet and making what sounded like dry heaves. "Oh, Casey ..." DJ gently placed a hand on her back. "I'm sorry."

Casey stood up and looked at DJ with bloodshot eyes. "I already threw up everything in my stomach." She gasped. "But I can't stop from—" She turned and did it again.

DJ got a glass of water and a damp washcloth and waited for Casey to stop. "Maybe if you drink a little water?" she suggested.

Casey frowned at the glass, then shook her head. "I can't."

"Here." DJ handed her the washcloth. "Wipe down your face."

"I'm so miserable." Casey started crying. "I don't know what to do."

"You should see a doctor," DJ told her, although she had no idea if that would help or not. But how could it hurt?

"I can't." Casey went down on her knees now, holding onto the toilet as she dry heaved again.

"Oh, Casey." DJ felt seriously concerned. "I don't know how to help you."

"Let me try the water," Casey said hoarsely, reaching for the glass.

"Okay." DJ nodded. "Just little sips."

Casey drank the water slowly, and for a few minutes it seemed to help. Then suddenly she barfed again. DJ felt helpless.

"DJ," Taylor called from outside the door. "Can I come in?"

"No," Casey said weakly.

"I think I know what's going on," Taylor called back. "Come on, Casey, let me in. I might be able to help."

Casey looked at DJ with fearful eyes, but DJ just shrugged. "Maybe she can help you."

Casey's face was pale, her hair stringy, and she looked beaten. "Okay . . . just don't tell her."

"I promise."

Casey turned back to the toilet, and DJ opened the door.

"Rhiannon went up to modeling practice. She'll explain that you guys are going to be a little late," Taylor said quickly.

"Thanks."

"How is she?" Taylor nodded toward the toilet where Casey was dry heaving again.

"Sick."

"Yes, I can see that." Taylor frowned. "And I'm guessing it's not from a hangover."

"What makes you think that?" Casey asked as she turned around and reached for the damp washcloth, using it to wipe her mouth.

"Because I've had a feeling about you, Casey."

Casey tossed a slightly accusatory glance DJ's way, but said nothing.

"Okay, it's just a wild guess," Taylor continued. "But I had a friend back in California . . . Alyssa got pregnant when she was fifteen ... and I was around her early on ... and lately you've reminded me of her."

Casey covered her face with the washcloth and pressed it into her face.

"I could be wrong, Casey, but I think you're pregnant."

DJ pretended to be busy at the sink, dampening another washcloth and filling the water glass. Anything to avoid Taylor's eyes, since she knew she'd give it away.

"Did DJ tell you?" Casey demanded.

"No." Taylor's voice was firm. "She never said a word."

"Oh."

"Honest," DJ assured Casey. "I didn't."

"So, cut to the chase, Taylor." Casey looked up with sad, red-rimmed eyes. "You said you could help."

"I'll be right back," Taylor promised, then took off.

"You swear you didn't tell her?" Casey challenged.

"I swear." DJ held up her hand. "As God is my witness, I did not tell her."

"I guess it figures that Taylor's got a nose for trouble."

DJ couldn't help but laugh. And before long, Taylor returned with soda crackers and milk. "Just take a tiny bite of cracker, chew it thoroughly, then one tiny sip of milk."

Casey made a face, but cooperated. It took awhile for her to get a couple of crackers and half a glass of milk down, but at least she wasn't hugging the toilet. And eventually it seemed like it was working. No more dry heaves.

Casey stood up, but still looked shaky. "Thanks, Taylor."

"I think you should get into bed," DJ said as she helped to brace her.

"I'll grab the waste can just in case you feel like you're going to hurl," Taylor said as she followed.

They helped Casey into bed. Then Taylor set the crackers and milk on the bedside table, and DJ put a cool damp cloth over her forehead.

"Taylor?" whispered Casey.

"Yeah?"

"Please don't tell."

"I won't."

"You can trust her," DJ promised Casey. "She won't."

"Thanks."

"You get some rest," Taylor said kindly. "And we better get up to modeling practice before Mrs. Carter sends out a search crew."

As Taylor and DJ hurried upstairs to join the others, DJ wished she could tell Grandmother what was up. But she knew she couldn't break her promise to Casey. Still, it would be comforting to have an adult in this loop. Even if it was a loopy adult like her grandmother.

7

Last Dance

"IT'S nice TO see THAT YOU GIrLS COULD finally make it," Miss Walford announced loudly as DJ and Taylor slinked into the room. She reached over to turn off the music, then placed both hands on her hips and faced them with a dour expression. "I'm not sure how Mrs. Carter feels about tardiness, but it is one of my pet peeves. My time is valuable and right now I'm donating my free time, which makes it even more valuable. I don't appreciate you girls wasting it."

"I'm sorry," DJ began, "but Casey was really—"

"Rhiannon made your excuses." Miss Walford's tone was skeptical. "But unless it was a serious medical emergency— and I didn't hear any ambulances arrive—I hardly think it was necessary for both of you to stay with her."

DJ glanced around for Grandmother, but didn't see her.

"Shall we assume that Casey is all right?"

"She's resting," Taylor said crisply.

"Oh, good. So perhaps you're ready to join us now?"

"Of course."

"Get in line," Miss Walford commanded. "And I mean the *end* of the line, girls."

71

Some of the others, including Madison and Tina, snickered as Taylor and DJ went to the end of the line.

Taylor tossed DJ a nonchalant glance, and DJ rolled her eyes as if to say "Whatever." But as they practiced, it was clear that Miss Walford's battle lines were drawn. DJ and Taylor had definitely made her black list and, judging by her snide comments and criticisms, it wasn't going to change anytime soon. DJ wondered what Grandmother would say about this—or if she'd even find out. Not that DJ cared particularly. It was Miss Walford's choice to act like a spoiled brat. And maybe that helped to explain why girls like Madison and Tina acted the way they did. Maybe they were just imitating their dance team coach.

With only one week left, Eliza grew even more determined to win votes for prom queen. DJ wondered if it was Eliza's way of making up for not being accepted to Yale or if it was something more. Because, although DJ hadn't been paying really close attention, Eliza seemed different. Like she was supercharged or taking enhancement drugs (like an athlete on steroids), or had simply been drinking too much coffee. But it was like the girl never slowed down or ran out of energy. Eliza never seemed to stop. Kind of like that obnoxious pink Energizer Bunny, Eliza never stopped moving and talking and smiling. Not only that, but she suddenly seemed very helpful and concerned about everyone and anyone. DJ wasn't sure if it was sincere or just more campaigning. It felt as if winning prom queen was the most important triumph in the universe.

Even so, DJ kept her promise and campaigned for her. Sure, it was a little halfhearted. But it was hard to feign enthusiasm for handing out silly pink buttons, T-shirts, and chocolates. Besides that, she wondered who really cared. Other than snarfing down free chocolate, it seemed pretty pointless. And yet DJ was occasionally surprised that some of her friends took her endorsement for Eliza seriously.

"She's really changed, hasn't she?" Monica Bradford said to DJ as she pinned a button to the collar of her denim jacket.

"Hopefully we all change," DJ said lightly. "I mean, as in growing up."

"Anyway, Eliza seems a lot nicer now than she was at the beginning of the year." Monica lowered her voice. "She was such a snob then. But now she smiles and says hi to everyone."

DJ nodded. "She's definitely gotten friendlier." Of course, DJ still suspected Eliza's goodwill was only skin deep, an effort to win votes, but who was she to judge? Maybe Eliza really had changed. No one could deny that she'd been different since Palm Beach.

"Well, she's got my vote," Monica assured DJ.

"Thanks!"

"I *was* going to vote for Haley Callahan."

"Oh ..." DJ wasn't sure she wanted to go there. Despite the rough history she'd had with Monica and Haley back during swim team season, Haley was a friend now.

"But Haley has changed. It's like she's all stuck-up now."

"Really?" DJ frowned. "I hadn't noticed."

"Probably because she's nice to you. But she's picky about who she's nice to. Not like you." Monica picked up a Queen Eliza bumper sticker. "And not like Eliza."

"Well, I know Eliza will appreciate your support," DJ told Monica. In fact, Eliza would be relieved to know that she'd just gotten what could've been a Haley vote. Eliza was certain that Haley was her biggest competition in the race for the crown. Oh, Madison had her friends, but she had her enemies too. Mostly Eliza had been concerned about the three-way split on votes. And just last night, she'd actually been trying to think of a way to buy out Haley.

"You can't do that," DJ had told Eliza after she'd disclosed her latest campaign strategy. She wanted to get her dad to contribute money to Haley's college fund in exchange for Haley dropping out of the race.

"Why not?" Eliza had looked honestly surprised. "I thought Haley would appreciate some tuition money."

"Because that's like *buying* your crown," DJ had told her.

"So?" Eliza had shrugged. "That's how politicians get elected."

DJ had just rolled her eyes. "Look, Eliza, it'll be a lot more rewarding if you win the election fair and square."

Fortunately, Eliza had seemed to get this. Or mostly. "Okay, DJ, but you better keep helping me."

And that was why DJ was stuck at the campaign table throughout the lunch hour today. Conner had felt sorry for her and was coming back to sit with her after he grabbed them both some tacos. DJ turned, thinking that he was tapping on her shoulder. But it was Rhiannon and she looked worried.

"We have a problem!" she hissed.

"What?"

"Casey ..." Rhiannon glanced around as if to be sure no one was eavesdropping.

"What about Casey?" DJ felt worried. As far as she knew, Rhiannon was still in the dark about Casey's pregnancy, but what if Casey was sick again?

"Casey just told me that someone made a MySpace page about Eliza."

"Oh." DJ felt a small wave of relief. "So what's the problem?"

"Remember when Casey slandered Taylor online last fall?"

"Oh no." DJ's hand flew to her mouth. "Did Casey do it again? Please, tell me she didn't. She cannot possibly be that—"

"No, no—that's not it. Casey just happened to find it during her graphic design class. And now it seems that everyone is finding it. Casey is actually trying to get the thing shut down, but apparently that's not so easy."

"What's on the page?"

"It's about Palm Beach."

"Palm Beach?"

"It's this overblown story about how Eliza hooked up with this criminal boyfriend in order to fake her own kidnapping so that she could extort money from her family's fortune. But it's really bad, and there are some skanky photos of Eliza that must've been done through Photoshop."

DJ tipped her head back and moaned.

"Should we do something?"

"Does Eliza know about it yet?" DJ glanced over to where Eliza was smiling and shaking hands with "fans," totally oblivious to the storm that was brewing.

"Doesn't look like it."

Just then DJ noticed a fringe of onlookers who were quietly pointing toward Eliza and snickering like they were in on the secret joke. "It's just a matter of time."

"What do we do?"

DJ thought for a moment. What did they do last time this happened? "Damage control." She stood up. "You go to administration and tell them what's going on and see if they can help. I'll give Eliza a heads-up."

"Right."

DJ hurried over to where Eliza was handing goodie bags to some freshman girls with starry eyes. "Eliza," DJ said quietly.

"Just a minute, please," Eliza said sweetly. "And you girls don't forget to vote on Friday. Who knows, maybe it'll be one of you in a few years." The girls giggled and moved on.

"Eliza, you *need* to listen to me," DJ said urgently. "Something's wrong."

Eliza's turned to face DJ. "What?"

DJ whispered the news about the MySpace page, watching as Eliza's smile faded.

"Seriously?" Eliza's blue eyes grew concerned. "Have you seen it?"

"I didn't, but Casey—"

"Did Casey do this?"

"No, of course not. She's the one who told Rhiannon to tell me. In fact, I think she's doing what she can to shut the thing down. And Rhiannon went to the administration office to tell them. I just thought you should know."

Eliza turned around and grabbed her oversized Versace bag. Slipping out her slender laptop, she popped it open, did a quick search, and found the page. DJ watched over her shoulder. The page really was sick. DJ felt a mixture of anger and disgust. Then she noticed that Eliza's face was pale and her hands were trembling. She snapped her computer shut and struggled to shove it back into her bag. "Will you walk with me to my car, DJ?"

"Of course." But as DJ escorted her out of the cafeteria, she noticed that Eliza seemed to be weaving, almost as if she were intoxicated.

"Are you okay?" DJ asked. When Eliza didn't answer, DJ grasped her elbow and, instead of walking her to the parking lot, DJ turned toward the counseling center and went directly to Mrs. Seibert's office.

"Hello, girls." The counselor looked up from a bag lunch on her desk. "To what do I owe this—"

"It's Eliza, Mrs. Seibert." DJ spoke quickly as she eased Eliza into a chair, where she slumped forward like a rag doll. "I think she needs help."

Mrs. Seibert blinked, then looked from one girl to the next. "What's wrong? Does she need medical treatment?"

DJ didn't know how much to say, so she quickly launched into the story of the MySpace page.

"Oh, is that what Mr. Van Duyn is working on? I heard we have another Internet scandal going on. So juvenile."

DJ nodded. "Yeah. But there's a little more to it than that." She put her hand on Eliza's shoulder. "Do you mind if I tell her about Palm Beach, Eliza? I mean, she's a counselor, so you know she'll keep it confidential."

"I ... don't ... care ..." Eliza's voice was weak.

So DJ sat down and, as gently as possible, told Mrs. Seibert about the kidnapping that had happened in Palm Beach, as well as how her grandmother had asked for the girls not to talk about it. "So it's just been kind of swept under the rug ... until today."

"Oh, my goodness!" Mrs. Seibert's eyebrows arched high. "What a horror story. Poor Eliza. No wonder she's upset."

"And it seems like Eliza should've been to a shrink or something," DJ continued. "In fact, that's what a counselor told us in Palm Beach. But that hasn't happened."

Mrs. Seibert shook her head sadly. "DJ, if you'll excuse us, I'd like to talk to Eliza privately."

"No problem." DJ stood quickly, eager to get out of there. "Thanks." As she walked back to the cafeteria, she prayed for Eliza. And she prayed that Mrs. Seibert would have some good advice and some good resources.

"Hey, what happened to you?" Conner asked when she rejoined him at the campaign table.

"You mean you didn't hear yet?"

He shook his head and she filled him in.

"Man." He slapped down the neatly stacked bumper stickers with a loud smack. "I cannot believe what some girls will do. Seriously, DJ, I don't think guys would do something like that."

"Most girls wouldn't either."

"Yeah . . . you're probably right."

"Anyway, it really hit a nerve with Eliza. She just kind of unraveled and fell apart."

"Is she going to be okay?"

"She's with the counselor now. And that's probably a good thing."

"So now we'll really have to do some top-notch campaigning." Conner waved to a couple of his soccer buddies. "Come on over here," he called. And before they could protest, Conner was pinning pink buttons onto their shirts. "Eliza Wilton really needs your support," he told them in a serious tone, "more than ever now."

"Was that MySpace page stuff true?" one of the guys asked DJ. She thought his name was James.

"No way." DJ firmly shook her head. "It was just some lowlife's attempt to smear Eliza's name. And it was downright mean. She's really hurting because of it."

"Too bad." James looked exasperated. "Well, Eliza's got my vote now."

DJ felt a slight glimmer of hope. Maybe this scam plan would backfire. Maybe it would invoke sympathy for Eliza. Still, DJ wondered who had done it. Madison seemed the strongest suspect. And yet, Haley had done something similar to DJ last year, using her cell phone to send mean messages. So who knew? And maybe it didn't really matter. Maybe it would actually provide the catalyst for Eliza to get some help. And DJ felt certain that Eliza needed help.

**8**

*Last Dance*

"DJ, YOU HAVE TO HELP ME!" Eliza's voice sounded urgent over the phone.

"What's happening? Where are you?" DJ and the other Carter House girls had gone out to the school parking lot and noticed that Eliza's car was gone. "We've been looking all over for you."

"Mrs. Seibert sent me home. But not until she called my mother."

"Oh?"

"She told her the whole story and my mother totally freaked."

"That's kind of understandable, Eliza."

"I suppose ... but now Mom's on her way over here. Well, not here-here, but to Louisville. I'm at the airport right now, waiting for a four o'clock flight so I can meet Mom at home — and hopefully smooth this thing out."

DJ grimaced to think of how her grandmother must be feeling about all this. To find out that Eliza had deceived her by not informing her parents about Palm Beach, combined with the humiliation of the Wiltons possibly blaming Grandmother

79

for being irresponsible, well, it wouldn't be pretty. "You said you needed my help," DJ reminded her.

"That's right, I do!"

"But what — "

"I need you to smooth things out with Mrs. Carter, DJ." Eliza was talking fast again, but her voice sounded shaky. "I need you to make her realize that it's okay for me to come back to Crescent Cove. And I need her to help me convince my mom that everything's fine. You're the only one who can do this. Do you understand?"

"I guess . . . I mean, if it's even possible."

"Besides that I need you guys to keep my campaign for prom queen going. I already left a message for Daisy to keep everything like normal. There are only four days until the election and — "

"Do you seriously think you'll be back in time for — "

"I *have* to be back! You know how much this means to me!"

DJ wanted to point out that being crowned prom queen seemed minor compared to everything else at the moment, but she was pretty sure that would hurt Eliza's feelings.

"Are you still there, DJ?"

"Yes."

"So you'll do that for me?"

DJ made a desperate face toward her friends as they waited with curious faces. "I'll try. I mean, I can't promise results. But I'll do my best."

"I know you will." Eliza's voice smoothed out now. "I knew I could trust you."

DJ wanted to tell Eliza her plan sounded not only hopeless but slightly nutty as well, but she couldn't. "So . . . how are you feeling?" she asked hesitantly.

"I'm fine."

This didn't sound believable to DJ. "Really? You seemed pretty undone at noon."

"I think I was in shock."

"Yeah, that makes sense. By the way, Casey and Rhiannon managed to get that page removed from MySpace, and Mr. Van Duyn lodged a complaint and has already started interviewing the suspects."

"Good. And if they catch whoever did it—either Madison or Haley—maybe the election will change to a two-way split and help me to win."

DJ could not believe Eliza was so stuck on this. "Are you sure you're up for the stress, Eliza? You seemed really upset and—"

"Mrs. Seibert says it's just PTSD."

"Huh?"

"Post-Traumatic Stress Disorder."

"Seriously?"

"She gave me a booklet to read."

"Well, you should read it."

"I started to and I have it with me. I'm actually hoping I can use it as ammo against my mom. But, hey, they're starting to load first class now, so I better go. But promise me you'll do what I asked, okay?"

"I promise to do what I can."

"And I'll see you in a couple of days."

"Yeah . . ." DJ felt doubtful. "Have a good flight." They hung up and DJ just looked at her friends.

"What's going on?" Taylor demanded.

DJ gave them a quick rundown. "Despite everything, Eliza is determined to be back for prom."

"Good for her," Taylor said.

"Huh?" DJ felt confused.

"It might be good for her to finish this thing. Otherwise it'll be like Madison or whoever did that page won and like Eliza ran away scared."

DJ wasn't so sure. "Well, Eliza wants everyone to keep working on her campaign." DJ pointed to Taylor. "And I'm enlisting you to help me talk to my grandmother. We'll have to get her support for Eliza to come back."

"No problem."

"Hey, Casey!" called a guy's voice. They all turned to see Seth jogging toward the parking lot and waving. "Wait up."

DJ tried not to act irritated as Seth came over and faced Casey in what seemed a threatening way. "I thought you were going to wait for me, Casey."

"I wanted to make sure Eliza was okay," she answered stiffly.

"Then why was your phone turned off?" he challenged.

She shrugged. "Because we're not supposed to have it on during school hours?"

"FYI. School's out, Casey."

She shrugged again. "I was worried about Eliza, okay?"

He laughed. "Yeah, right."

DJ stepped next to Casey. "I'm heading home now. Case, are you ready to go?"

"I'll give her a ride," Seth said.

"Casey?" DJ locked eyes with her, but Casey just turned away.

"I can ride with Seth," she said quietly.

"Are you sure?"

Seth glared at DJ. She could only imagine what he wanted to say to her. She knew what she'd like to say to him. Instead, she just glared back.

"See you girls around," he called casually. Then he reached for Casey's arm and led her over to where his car was parked near the street.

"He is really starting to bug me," DJ said once they got into her car.

"*Starting to?*" Taylor ventured.

"Why does Casey put up with him?" Kriti asked from the backseat.

"Good question," Rhiannon said.

DJ just bit her lip and drove. But as she drove, she prayed for both Casey and Eliza. Both girls seemed headed down a crash course. DJ prayed that both of them would wake up and figure things out before it was too late.

"I appreciate your concern for Eliza," Grandmother told Taylor and DJ as they sat in the sitting area of her bedroom suite. "But I don't see that I can do anything about the situation." She frowned as she fingered the edge of a pale green silk scarf. "Eliza was dishonest with me and now her mother is furious. I can hardly imagine that Mrs. Wilton will agree to allow Eliza to return to Crescent Cove."

"Not even for graduation?" DJ asked.

Grandmother just shook her head.

"But Eliza *wants* to come back," Taylor persisted, "and it would probably be *good* for her to come back."

Then Taylor launched into her theory about how Eliza shouldn't let them beat her.

"That's right," agreed DJ. "It's like she's being punished twice. First she gets hurt in Palm Beach and now she has to miss out on prom and graduation as a result. That's just not fair."

"And what about the Mother's Day fashion show?" ventured Taylor. "It seems like Mrs. Wilton should want to come and watch Eliza participate in that."

Grandmother nodded sadly. "Yes, it does, doesn't it?"

"So can't you at least try to talk to her mom?" DJ pleaded.

"For Eliza's sake," added Taylor.

"Eliza will be miserable if she doesn't get to come back here." DJ stood. "If you really care about her, Grandmother, you'll do what you can to help her now."

"Of course I care about her."

"Then help her."

Grandmother closed her eyes and sighed in a slow, tired way. "I keep asking myself why I ever decided to take on all these girls ... why I ever thought I could do something like this ... what I must've been thinking ..." The way she spoke sounded like she was talking to herself.

DJ and Taylor exchanged glances.

"And at my age ... what made me assume I could be of any use to wild, young girls? Some of my friends have accused me of being insane. Some said I'd bitten off more than I could chew. Even the general has questioned me at times. Maybe they're all right ... maybe I am—"

"It hasn't been easy for you." DJ went over to stand by her grandmother, placing a hand on her shoulder. "But I know you really care about us. And I don't think you should blame yourself for everything. I mean, some of the girls have made some bad choices, but they'd probably do the same thing if they were home with their parents. Maybe even worse."

Grandmother's eyes opened wide.

"I have to agree with DJ, Mrs. Carter," Taylor said firmly.

"It's not your fault that teenage girls can make messes of their lives, Grandmother," DJ said defensively. "We see girls at school who live in perfectly normal homes and they do stupid things too."

Grandmother looked surprised. "Do they?"

"Of course." Taylor nodded. "And I was doing some pretty stupid things before I even came here. And look at me now—I'm doing much better."

"Yes, you are." Grandmother smiled slightly.

"And how about Rhiannon," DJ added. "She had no place to go and you made her feel welcome."

Grandmother stood now. "That reminds me. Some things arrived today." She rubbed her hands together eagerly. "I haven't told her yet, but Rhiannon's been accepted to the Fashion Institute of Technology—*with a full scholarship.*"

DJ let out a happy squeal. "Oh, that's fantastic!"

"See," Taylor told her. "You must know that never could've happened if you hadn't been helping her."

Grandmother nodded. "Yes, that's true."

"Rhiannon's going to be over the moon!"

"I want to surprise her at dinner," Grandmother said with renewed excitement. "I already asked Clara to make something special for dessert. So you girls don't tell her."

"And you'll call Eliza's mother?" DJ asked hopefully.

"In the morning." Grandmother stood straighter. "That will give her and Eliza a chance to talk ... a chance for things to calm down a bit."

DJ hugged her. "Thanks!"

"And the other things that arrived today were for you two girls. They came via FedEx from New York."

"Dylan's dresses?" Taylor asked hopefully.

"They're in your room." She looked from DJ to Taylor, then back at DJ. "Thank you for that little pep talk, girls. I needed it."

"Thank you," said DJ.

"And don't let the cat out of the bag with Rhiannon," Grandmother reminded them as they left.

As it turned out, the packages from New York didn't contain the dresses. But they did contain the shoes and fabric swatches.

"These are fabulous," Taylor said as she strutted around in the suede burgundy Jimmy Choo T-strap sandals.

"The note says that Dylan is working out a deal with Jimmy Choo," DJ said. "They'll be in his next show."

"Yay for Dylan!"

"And he needs us to take these shoes back with us when we go to New York this summer."

"No problem." Taylor came over to admire DJ's metallic silver sandals. "Aren't you going to try them on? They're gorgeous."

DJ glanced at her dirty flip-flop–shod feet and shook her head. "Not yet."

Taylor laughed. "I'm sure the Jimmy Choos appreciate that." She looked more closely at DJ's feet and made a face. "Man, you are so in need of a good pedicure."

"It just hasn't made my priority list."

"Well, you better get it on there before Saturday." Then she strutted off to the bathroom as if she were walking down the runway.

Soon, there was a knock on the door.

"Come in," DJ called as she put the lid back on the shoe box.

Rhiannon came in, holding up a sparkly dress in various shades of orange. "Have you heard from Casey? We were supposed to do a fitting today, and Kriti said she hasn't seen her yet."

DJ frowned when she glanced at the clock by her bed, which showed it was almost five. "If Seth was just bringing her home, you'd think she'd be here by now."

"Maybe they went for coffee or something," Taylor called from the bathroom.

DJ looked more closely at the dress in Rhiannon's hands. "Hey, this is really pretty."

"Thanks—I wanted to get it hemmed today. I still have to finish mine." Rhiannon noticed the shoe box on DJ's bed. "Jimmy Choos?" she said in surprise.

"Dylan sent them for us, along with fabric swatches for our dresses."

"Oh, please, let me see!" Rhiannon begged.

As DJ opened the box and peeled back the tissue, Rhiannon gushed, "Oh, DJ, that shade of aqua is going to be gorgeous on you!" She took out the shoes and held them up. "Oh, these are so beautiful."

"And see mine," Taylor said as she emerged from the bathroom to model her shoes.

"I can't wait to see the dresses—did Dylan send sketches?"

"No," DJ told her. "I guess he wants to surprise us. The dresses are supposed to be here by Friday."

"Wow, that's cutting it close."

"I don't think Dylan will let us go to the prom with only shoes and swatches," Taylor said in a teasing tone as she held up her fabric as if it were a tiny wine-colored dress.

DJ laughed. "Like that's going to happen."

Rhiannon sighed as she reverently set DJ's fabric swatch back with the shoes. "I just *love* fashion."

"We've noticed."

Rhiannon looked sad. "But I'm worried that God might be trying to tell me something."

"Huh?" DJ was confused.

"About what?" Taylor asked.

"Maybe it's too shallow to want to be a designer. I mean, there are people starving in the world and—"

"Some of the best designers donate lots of money to help those in need," Taylor pointed out. "I just read an article in *Vogue* that said they donated—"

"But maybe it's wrong for *me* to want to do something like that."

"Like what?" DJ asked. "Donate money?"

"No, not that. But maybe it's wrong that I want to work in something as superficial and shallow as fashion."

"Why is that wrong?" demanded Taylor. "Because you *love* it and because you're *good* at it? What if God gave you a special gift like that for a reason?"

"What kind of reason?" Rhiannon looked hopefully at Taylor.

"So you could design something fantastic for me to model?" Taylor chuckled.

Rhiannon frowned. "See what I mean ... shallow."

"So do you think it's shallow for me to want to model?" Taylor asked.

Rhiannon considered this. "Not if you remain true to yourself, Taylor. As long as you don't compromise your values, I don't think it's wrong."

"And what if Taylor became a positive influence," DJ suggested. "What if she's successful in modeling and stays strong in her faith and makes smart choices, and as a result there are girls who follow her career, girls who see her as a role model ... wouldn't that be pretty cool?"

"That would be awesome," Rhiannon agreed.

"And what's wrong with making great-looking clothes?" Taylor continued. "Do you think God wants us to go around looking like bag ladies?"

Rhiannon laughed. "No, I don't think God wants us to look like bag ladies. In fact, there's a place in the Bible, in Proverbs thirty-one, with a really great description of a godly woman who makes fine clothes for herself and her family and even enough to sell to others."

"See, there you go," DJ told her.

"I guess I'm just getting worried that it's not going to happen ... I mean, like I want it to happen. And I know I should be happy to go to NYU. And I can get into their design program and—"

"Maybe you just need to have more faith," Taylor told her with a perfectly straight face. "Give the whole thing to God and ask him to take care of it for you."

"That's what I've been trying to do."

"Just keep doing it," DJ said with her back toward Rhiannon, afraid her face was going to ruin her Grandmother's surprise.

**9**

*Last Dance*

"**I wonder if Casey's okay.**" DJ was sitting at the window seat, watching the street and worrying. Remembering Seth in the school parking lot gave her a bad feeling in the pit of her stomach.

Taylor looked up from her laptop. "Why wouldn't she be?"

"Seth."

"I'll be the first to admit, Seth's a piece of work, but I don't think there's any reason to ..." Taylor's brow creased. "What was his reaction to the pregnancy?"

DJ hadn't repeated anything that Casey had told her. She wasn't sure that just because Taylor *knew* meant that it was okay to disclose more.

"Let me guess," Taylor ventured. "Seth is really ticked. A pregnant girlfriend will mess up his life"—she switched to baby talk—"and his parents will get weelly mad and paddle his behind and take his wittle wed sports car away and cut back his allowance and—"

"Enough." DJ was laughing. "Yeah, something like that."

"So ... I'll bet Seth wants Casey to get an abortion."

DJ just shrugged.

"But ... let's see ... Casey isn't so sure about this. Her parents are strong Christians, so they probably oppose abortion. And yet Casey isn't so firm in her faith anymore. Plus, she doesn't want her parents to totally disown her either. So ... it could go either way."

"You know, if the modeling thing doesn't work out for you, you should join the CIA or something."

Taylor chuckled.

DJ picked up her phone. "I'm going to call her."

"It's a free country."

DJ was surprised when Casey answered, although it didn't quite sound like her. "Casey?"

"Yeah."

"Where are you?"

"In the bathroom."

"In the *bathroom*?"

Casey sniffed. "Is there a law against answering the phone in the bathroom?"

"No, of course not. What's up?"

"Nothing."

"So where are you? I mean, besides 'in the bathroom'? Who's bathroom is it?"

There was a long pause.

"Casey, are you there?"

"I'm at the Women's Health Center," she said quietly.

DJ considered this. "The Women's Health Center? Is that like a doctor's office?"

"Yes."

Taylor gave DJ a curious look.

"Is everything okay?" DJ asked. Casey didn't answer, but DJ could tell she was crying. Taylor was writing something on a piece of notebook paper. She held it out for DJ to see: *Abortion Central*.

"Are you getting an abortion?" DJ asked Casey.

"I—uh—I don't know."

"Is Seth with you?"

"In the bathroom?"

"No, at the Women's Health Center."

"He's waiting."

"Casey, what are you doing there?"

"I gotta go, DJ."

"Wait!"

But Casey had already hung up. DJ turned to Taylor. "Do you think that's what she's doing?"

Taylor just sighed and nodded.

"She was crying."

Taylor looked concerned. "Crying?"

"Yeah, she sounded really upset."

"Let's go." Taylor grabbed her bag. "My Vespa or your car?"

"My car."

DJ drove as fast as felt safe and soon they were quietly storming the Women's Health Center waiting room. They spotted Seth sitting in a corner, reading a magazine like he thought he was waiting to see the dentist.

"Where is Casey?" DJ demanded.

Seth looked up with alarm, then tried to act cool. "None of your business."

"We'll find her," Taylor said as she headed for the bathroom.

And they did find her, huddled on the floor of the bathroom, crying. DJ went down on her knees and wrapped her arms around Casey. "Oh, Casey, are you okay?"

Casey's shoulders shook as she began to cry harder.

"What is wrong with these people?" Taylor demanded. "They let a girl come in here and have a total breakdown and don't even come in to check?"

"Did you have it already?" DJ asked quietly.

Casey looked up with puffy eyes. "Have what?"

"The abortion."

Casey shook her head, then buried her face in her knees again.

DJ and Taylor exchanged glances.

"Are you going to have an abortion?" Taylor asked.

Casey didn't answer.

"Talk to us, Casey," pleaded DJ. "We're here to help. What's going on?"

Casey looked up again. "I—I had a—an examination. And it was horrible. And I'm supposed to schedule another—another appointment."

"You don't have to do anything you don't want to do," DJ told her.

"But I—I have to—to take care of this," Casey sputtered. "It's my responsibility."

"That's true," Taylor said as she extended her hand to help her up. "The baby is your responsibility. But you don't have to make this decision today."

"Right." DJ stood and offered Casey her other hand.

"Come on," Taylor urged. "Let's get out of here."

"And unless you want to go out there and deal with Seth, we're taking you home," DJ informed her.

"But he'll be mad."

"Let him be mad," Taylor said.

"Yeah," agreed DJ. "Let him show you what he's made of."

"And what he's full of," added Taylor.

Then, with Taylor and DJ flanking Casey, they marched through the waiting room. When the woman at the desk tried to stop them, Taylor faced her down. "Our friend is confused and upset and wants to leave," Taylor said firmly.

"But she needs to see the—"

"Are you saying you won't allow Casey to leave?" Taylor demanded. "Because I can get an attorney in here like *that*." She snapped her fingers in the startled woman's face. "I don't think you want to be accused of holding a juvenile here against her will, do you? That might make for an interesting news story. Would you like me to call the press?"

The woman backed down, and the three continued through the waiting area, totally ignoring Seth, who had already tossed down his magazine to follow them out to the car. Before they could get Casey into the front seat, Seth was trying to intervene.

"What did you do to her?" he demanded.

"Wouldn't that be more like what *you* did to her?" Taylor shot back at him.

"I'm helping her," he said.

"You're helping yourself," DJ told him as she eased Casey into the passenger seat, then closed the door.

"Casey!" He slammed his fist on the roof of the car. "You get out of there and come with me!"

She didn't even look up.

"Leave her alone," DJ said.

"She is not going to have that baby!" he yelled.

"That's not for you to decide," Taylor said as she closed the door behind Casey.

"That baby is half mine," he declared, "and my half is not—"

"Not what?" DJ got close to his face. "Not going to live? What are you going to do, Seth, kill half a baby? You don't think that would be murder?"

He didn't answer.

"Take a hike, Seth," Taylor said as she got into the backseat.

"And unless you plan to grow up real soon, just leave Casey alone." DJ got into the car, started the engine, and began to back out. But there was a loud noise and the whole car shook.

"Did I run over him?" DJ stepped on the brake in panic.

"No, that moron just kicked your car."

DJ put the car into park and got out in time to see Seth stomping toward his car. And sure enough, he *had* kicked her car. Right there on the passenger side where Casey was sitting was a big indentation. DJ just shook her head as she got back into the car. "Seth is a maniac," she said quietly.

Casey was crying again. And DJ's hands shook as she drove home. She didn't think they were in any real danger, but it was upsetting just the same. She wondered if she should tell her grandmother about how her car had gotten damaged or just hope that she didn't notice. DJ parked the car in the driveway, and they all got out to examine the foot-sized dent.

"I'm sorry," Casey muttered, "this is all my fault."

"It is not your fault," DJ said.

"That's right," Taylor agreed. "It's Seth's fault. And if you have the sense I think you have, you'll drop that boy like a hot potato."

Casey nodded.

"It's almost dinnertime," DJ said as they went inside. "Let's put on our party faces, because Grandmother has a special announcement tonight."

"That's right," Taylor said. "Casey, you come into our room and splash some cold water on your face, and I'll help you with some makeup."

Before long, Casey's puffy eyes and red face were just a memory, and all three girls made it down in time for dinner. Although Casey was even quieter than usual, no one seemed to notice since Rhiannon was the woman of the hour. She was ecstatic to hear Grandmother's good news. And when Inez and Clara came in with not only a cake but a bottle of sparkling cider as well, Rhiannon cried tears of joy.

"You are all so wonderful," she said as they all held up their flutes of sparkling cider. "I feel like God gave me a family when he allowed me to be part of Carter House. And I am so thankful."

"Here's to Rhiannon," Grandmother said. "To her success at the Fashion Institute of Technology and to her future in the fashion world."

"To Rhiannon!" they echoed.

By Wednesday afternoon, it seemed that Eliza's slightly impaired race for the crown was about to come to a screeching halt. But it wasn't from a lack of trying on the part of the Carter House girls. Even Casey, who, thanks to Seth, was bluer than blue, was doing her best to help out.

"It's hopeless," DJ confessed to Eliza's supporters as they gathered in a quiet nook of the locker bay for a quick after-school meeting.

"Why?" Daisy demanded.

"For one thing, it's not looking like Eliza's mother is going to let her come back," DJ explained. "Besides that, no one's been able to figure out who made the MySpace page, so both

Madison and Haley are still solidly in the race. And besides that, there's a new rumor circulating about Eliza."

"What?" Daisy frowned.

"You haven't heard it?" Kriti asked.

"No, what is it?"

"People are saying that Eliza made the MySpace page herself just to get the others in trouble and to garner sympathy from the voters," Taylor said.

"That's nuts!" Daisy shook her fist. "Certifiably nuts."

"Yes," DJ told her. "We agree. But for some reason, people are buying it. And Eliza not being here to defend herself seems to add fuel to their fire."

"So are you going to quit campaigning completely?" Daisy asked.

DJ frowned. "I really don't see the point in dragging this out."

"Especially if she's not coming back," added Rhiannon.

"It's feeling pretty lame," Casey said quietly.

"Having a campaign meeting, are we?" Madison asked coyly as she and Tina paused to stare at the small gathering.

"Get a life," Daisy called back at them.

But they just laughed and continued walking.

"See," DJ said, "what's the point in prolonging this losing battle?"

"When did you last talk to Eliza?" asked Daisy.

"At noon." DJ shook her head. "She sounded depressed. She was on her way to the shrink, and it seemed perfectly clear that her mother was not budging."

"It's so unfair." Daisy slammed her fist into a locker.

"Easy, girl," Taylor said.

"Hey, maybe you'd like to run as a write-in," DJ said to Daisy, "in Eliza's place."

Daisy shook her head. "No, thanks."

"Okay, then." DJ wanted to wrap this up. "I think we need to let it go. I mean, if anyone wants to keep campaigning, go ahead, but I'm pretty sure it's hopeless."

"I'm going to call her," Daisy announced as she opened her phone. They all waited until Daisy had Eliza on the other end. "So, what are the chances of you making it back here?" she asked hopefully. She waited and her face grew cloudy. "Really?" Her mouth twisted downward. "Oh, I'm sorry, Eliza." She just shook her head. "Well, you hang in there, okay?" Then Daisy hung up and looked at the rest of them with a hopeless expression. "DJ's right. It's over."

"Sorry to run," Kriti told them, "but Josh is waiting."

"And I promised to run Rhiannon to the fabric store," Taylor told them.

Rhiannon grinned. "On her Vespa, which will be a first for me."

"So, just for clarity," DJ said quickly, "we're quitting the campaign?"

Everyone seemed to agree, but as they went their separate ways, DJ felt a sense of sadness and loss. Just before she left the locker bay, she glanced at a campaign poster of Eliza. A corner had come un-taped and DJ paused to re-adhere it to the window. She looked at Eliza's bright, smiling, confident face (a photo that DJ had found irritating a couple weeks ago) and realized that she actually missed the princess. More than that, she felt a sense of personal responsibility—Eliza had begged DJ to help her, but DJ had let her down. Still, DJ didn't know what more could be done. Grandmother had tried ... and it's not like they could force Eliza's mother to allow her to come back.

**10**

*Last Dance*

"WHAT A BEAUTIFUL DAY," DJ observed as she drove away from the school with Casey slouched in the passenger seat. "Makes me want to go to the beach."

"Go for it," Casey said in a flat tone.

"You want to?"

She just shrugged, but DJ took that for a yes and turned onto the beach road. Before long they both had their shoes off and were walking down the beach. Neither of them said much. They just strolled along, moving out of the way when a wave rolled in too quickly. Finally Casey got tired and they found a handy log to sit on.

"So ... how are you doing?" DJ asked.

"You mean besides being knocked up and recently dumped?"

"No ... I mean, that too."

"I've had better days."

"I know ..." DJ reached down and scooped up some cool sand in her hand, letting it trickle between her fingers as she wondered what she could possibly say to make Casey feel better.

There was a long silence ... the only sounds were the waves and a few gulls screeching.

"What would you do if you were me, DJ?"

DJ considered this. Well, for starters, she'd never be in that place ... or would she? She suddenly remembered those few times when she and Conner had pushed things a little far, times when she'd been tempted to go farther, and how they'd finally drawn some lines in their relationship. "I'm not sure what I'd do, Casey. But I think if my mom was alive, I'd tell her."

"But your mom was cool."

"Your mom's cool too, Casey."

"She's okay ... for a mom ... but she's so caught up in being a perfect church lady that I know she'll go to pieces if she finds out that I'm pregnant."

"You might be surprised."

"I doubt it."

"But you'll never know if you don't give her a chance, Casey."

"True ..."

"You know what?"

"What?"

"If I could trade places with you—I mean, if I could be pregnant and have my mom be alive so that I could tell her I was pregnant—I'd do it in a heartbeat."

Casey didn't say anything.

"I know that probably sounds lame, but it's true."

"I believe you."

"Is your mom coming for the Mother's Day fashion show?"

"I think so. She was trying to decide between that and graduation. She said they can't afford both."

"So if she comes ... would you tell her?"

Another long silence.

"You know what will happen if I tell her, DJ."

"What?"

"She'll insist that I keep the baby."

"Keep it as in *keep* it and raise it and everything?"

"No ... probably not like that. I mean as in *not* have an abortion."

"Would that be so bad?"

"You mean, go through a whole pregnancy and give birth to a baby?"

DJ grimaced. "When you put it like that it does sound a little overwhelming."

"Tell me about it."

"But I wonder how you'd feel if you didn't do that." DJ squinted up at the sky. "I mean ... if I were you, I wonder how I'd feel."

"How do you think you'd feel?"

"I think I'd feel sad."

Casey just nodded.

"And guilty." DJ sighed. "And I wonder if that sadness and guilt would last longer than nine months ... you know what I mean?"

"Like a lifetime?"

"I don't know."

"Would you hate me if I got an abortion?"

"No, of course not."

"But you'd be mad at me?"

DJ didn't know how to answer that. "I guess I'd be more concerned than mad. Like I'd want to know why you felt you had to do it. Like, was it your choice or was someone, like Seth, pressuring you? And I'd want to be sure you were really okay with it. Taylor and I saw how stressed-out you were at the abortion place—it seemed pretty obvious that you weren't feeling too good about it then."

"I was scared. And Seth wasn't helping."

"Seth was only thinking of Seth."

"I know that now." Casey picked up a stick and drew a circle in the sand. "And I also know he's already invited Jolene Kranz to the prom."

"Seriously?"

Casey nodded. "I don't really care. I know I'm better off without him."

"It's got to hurt."

"Oh, yeah ... it hurts."

"Hey, why don't you go to the prom with someone else too?"

Casey actually laughed.

"You could," DJ persisted.

"Right. Three days to find a prom date. Sounds like a bad summer movie."

"It could happen. In fact, we could make it happen."

"Thanks, but no thanks."

"So, you're saying you want to sit at home alone on prom night?"

Casey's mouth twisted.

"Think about it. Seth will be there with Jolene and you'll be home in your sweats and slippers feeling like a reject."

"Who's going to want to—"

"Can you trust me, Case?"

"Trust you to twist some guy's arm to—"

"No, I'll ask Conner if he knows someone. I mean, think about it. What if there's some nice guy who would love to go to prom but was too afraid to ask a girl, and now he regrets it and thinks it's too late."

Casey snickered.

"I'm glad I'm entertaining you."

"Yeah, thanks." Casey threw her stick over her shoulder. "Sure, knock yourself out, DJ, see if you can find some pathetic loser to take the jilted pregnant girl to the prom."

"No one *knows* you're pregnant."

"Not yet."

"Meaning?"

"I don't know." Casey stood up. "And maybe I don't even care. It's not like I've ever had a great reputation at that school anyway."

"Well, I seriously doubt that Seth will go shooting his mouth off. According to Taylor, he's worried about what mommy and daddy would do."

"That's the truth."

"And you can trust Taylor and me to keep quiet."

"I know I can trust you."

"You can trust Taylor too."

"So you say ..."

"Anyway, back to prom. If Conner finds a guy to go with you, you'll really cooperate? I don't want to set some nice guy up for a letdown."

"Just make sure Conner actually gets a *nice* guy." Casey stuck out her chin. "He doesn't even have to be a hunk ... as long as he's *nice.*"

"Wow." DJ nodded. "I'm impressed."

Casey let out a swear word.

"Okay, I take it back. I'm *not* impressed."

"No, that's not it ... I just remembered something. If I go to the prom, I'll have to go to youth group tonight. Otherwise I can't wear the dress Rhiannon made."

"That's right." DJ tried not to sound too smug. "But you have to admit that dress is totally worth it."

As they walked back to the car, Casey continued to grumble about the fairness of the dress exchange and whether or not she really wanted to go to the prom, and all the reasons why she should just forget the whole thing. "I mean, seriously," she said as DJ unlocked her car, "why bother? Life as I know it is over with anyway." Tears were coming down her cheeks. "I've messed up a lot, DJ, but this time I really did it."

DJ didn't know what to say.

"And even if I can undo my mess, I know that it'll never go away completely. I'll never be who I was before." Casey sniffed loudly. "I wish there were do-overs . . . or that I could turn back time."

"Yeah . . . I'm sure a lot of people feel that way." Now DJ wondered if her prom idea was really that great. Finding a pregnant friend a date to the prom seemed a little like putting a Band-Aid on a broken arm. Still, she felt sorry for Casey and was becoming increasingly concerned that she might slide into a really deep depression.

After they got home, DJ called Conner. "I need a big favor," she told him.

"What?"

"Can you find Casey a date for the prom?"

"Kinda short notice, isn't it?"

"Duh. But she's really bummed about Seth breaking up. And now he's taking Jolene Kranz, and if we could find Casey a date, well, it wouldn't be quite so painful."

"Don't you mean if *I* can find her a date?"

"Well, if you don't want—"

"Sorry . . . I was just jerking your chain."

"Thanks. Anyway, are we still on for youth group tonight?"

"Sure. Hey, do you think Casey would go for someone from youth group?"

"I don't know." DJ considered this. "Are you thinking of anyone specifically?"

"Not specifically."

"Well, I did promise her someone *nice*."

"Hey, Emery Klaus is nice."

DJ considered this. Emery was nice. But he was also extremely shy. And Casey would probably think he was kind of nerdish. And yet he *was* kind of cute and interesting ... and smart. "Yeah, Emery might work. But I wonder what he'd think about Casey. I mean, she's kind of mouthy sometimes and she's definitely not a Christian."

"Maybe he'd consider her a mission."

"Funny." DJ tried not to imagine Emery bringing his Bible to the prom and preaching to Casey. Not that Casey couldn't use some of that. But still ...

"Or maybe he'll just be interested because she's so different from him."

"They say opposites attract."

"Can't get more opposite than those two." He chuckled.

"And it's not like we're playing matchmaker, Conner. It's just that I can't bear the idea of Casey sitting home alone on prom night. She's already depressed enough thanks to — " She had to remind herself that Conner didn't know about the pregnancy.

"Casey should be happy to be rid of Seth. But I know that's not how it works."

"Unfortunately."

"I'll talk to Emery," he said. "Maybe I should call him first. Kind of give him a heads-up. You do the same with Casey. Then we can casually introduce them tonight."

"Sounds like a plan."

"Why don't we just meet at the church? That'll give me more time to talk to him."

"And I can sound out Casey."

"If this works, maybe we can start up a business."

"An emergency dating service."

He laughed. "See you tonight."

DJ closed her phone. Now all she had to do was to convince Casey that Emery would be a great date. But it wouldn't be easy. And, really, DJ had to ask herself again, was it even worth it? Especially considering the bigger issue going on. She decided to just pray about it. Hopefully God had a bigger, better plan. She prayed that he'd show them.

"What's up?" Taylor asked as she came into the room.

DJ told her about her concerns for Casey and what she and Conner were working on. Taylor just laughed.

"What's so funny?" DJ tried not to be offended.

"Sorry, but I can't think of anyone more totally the opposite of Seth Keller than Emery Klaus. Not that I think it's a bad thing. Just pretty funny."

"Yeah, and Casey will probably say 'Forget it.'"

Taylor got a thoughtful expression. "Unless we really give this some careful consideration . . ."

"How so?"

"Well . . ." Taylor was pacing now. Not that you could call it pacing; it was more like strutting. "What if we both act like Emery is all that and a bag of chips."

"All that and a bag of chips?" DJ frowned. "Huh?"

Taylor laughed. "It's something one of mom's roadies used to say."

"Oh, I think I get you. We act like Emery is hot, and Casey gets pulled in."

Now Taylor looked concerned. "But we need to make sure Emery doesn't get hurt. He's really a sweet guy."

"And he's so shy."

"But this might actually be good for him."

"It might be good for Casey too." DJ picked up her phone. "I want to let Conner in on our slight change of plans. He was expecting me to talk to Casey and get her kind of warmed up to the idea. But now we're going in cold turkey."

Taylor giggled as DJ called Conner and filled him in. "I know it sounds kind of crazy," she said finally, "but it might make this thing work."

"At least I'll know not to get jealous when I see you flirting with Emery."

"You can get jealous if you want." She laughed. "See ya later."

After DJ hung up, Taylor asked if she'd heard from Eliza.

"No, why?"

"I just wondered if she knows that we've given up on her campaign."

"I suppose someone should tell her," DJ admitted, "not that it should really matter. I mean, it's not like she's coming back."

"Not at all?"

"It sounded pretty hopeless when Daisy called her. Her mother is really digging in her heels."

"That seems so mean." Taylor shook her head. "I mean, who would've thought I'd ever come to Eliza's defense? But I do feel sorry for her."

"Me too." DJ picked up her phone, then set it down again. "I just can't bear to call her. Isn't that kind of like kicking someone when they're down?"

"Maybe."

"I wish there was something more I could do to help."

"I really thought your grandmother would be able to straighten it out."

"I did too."

"I mean, if they gave out awards for damage control, your grandmother would probably have a few by now."

DJ smiled. "Probably. But to be fair, a lot of times it's by default or even just pure luck."

"So have you talked to her about why Eliza can't come back?"

"Grandmother?"

"Yes. Did she say why Mrs. Wilton was being so stubborn?"

"No . . . but I didn't ask."

"Maybe you should."

DJ considered this. "Maybe so. That way I could tell Eliza that I really did give it my best shot." She stood up and dropped her phone on the bed. "Okay, here I go . . ."

"Want me to come for backup?"

DJ considered the offer. "No, I think one-on-one might be best."

Taylor nodded. "Good idea. That way she won't be on the defensive."

DJ made a praying gesture with her hands and Taylor nodded. Then, with very little hope, DJ went and knocked on her grandmother's door.

11

Last Dance

**"I DON'T rEaLLY WISH TO DISCUSS THIS,"** Grandmother said firmly.

DJ had just asked why Mrs. Wilton had refused to allow Eliza to come back to Crescent Cove. "But it makes no sense."

"Perhaps it doesn't make sense to you, DJ, but it probably makes perfect sense to Mrs. Wilton ... and to me."

"But what about prom and the fashion show and graduation?" DJ persisted. "Eliza will miss out on everything."

"It might be for the best."

"I can't believe you actually think that." DJ studied her grandmother. She was stretched out on her lounge chair with a copy of *Vogue* in her lap. "I thought you *cared* about Eliza."

The magazine slipped to the floor as Grandmother stood. "I do care about Eliza." She walked over to the window, her back to DJ.

"Then why won't you help her?"

Grandmother didn't answer.

"Did you even call her mother? Did you really try—"

"*Desiree!*" Grandmother turned and faced DJ with a withering look.

"But I—"

"Enough!" Grandmother went over to her bureau and jerked open a drawer. DJ wasn't sure whether to run or wait. Then Grandmother turned around with what appeared to be a Walgreen's bag in her hand. She held it out to DJ.

DJ took the bag and looked inside to see what appeared to be a used home pregnancy test. "Huh?"

"Inez gave this to me before I called Mrs. Wilton."

DJ closed the bag and pushed it back toward her grandmother. "I don't get it."

"Inez found it in Eliza and Rhiannon's bathroom trash can."

"Really?" DJ was stunned.

"Yes. I asked Rhiannon if it was hers."

"And she said no?"

Grandmother nodded with a somber expression.

"So you assumed it's Eliza's?"

"Who else?"

DJ didn't know what to say.

"According to Inez, the test was positive."

"Meaning?" DJ felt like she was on unstable ground here. Was it really possible that Eliza was pregnant too? How weird was that? Or was it more likely that Casey had ditched her home pregnancy kit in someone else's trash can?

"It seems obvious, Desiree. Eliza is pregnant."

"Did you ask her?"

"No ... I haven't spoken to Eliza."

"How about her mother? Did you ask her?"

"No." Grandmother looked appalled. "Do you seriously think I would ask Mrs. Wilton about something like this? I can only imagine what she must think of me … not only did her daughter suffer the … uh … the incident in Palm Beach, but now she's pregnant as well." Grandmother reached into her pocket to retrieve a handkerchief, and daubed her eyes with it. "I am so humiliated."

"But it's not your fault, Grandmother."

"I was the one in charge here," she said sadly. "This happened on my watch."

DJ didn't know what to say. But she had a strong suspicion the pregnancy kit did *not* belong to Eliza. "Can I use your phone?"

Grandmother looked puzzled. "Well, I don't know … I suppose."

DJ quickly called Eliza's cell phone and, to her relief, Eliza answered.

After a brief initial exchange, DJ jumped right in. "I need to ask you something."

"What?"

"Are you pregnant?"

"No, of course not! Good grief, DJ. Don't you think I have enough problems? Being pregnant would really be the icing on the cake. Why would you even ask—"

"Sorry, but Grandmother was under the impression you were."

"But why?"

"Never mind about that. Do you still want to come back for prom and everything?"

"I wish I could."

"Do you think it would help if Grandmother spoke to your mother?"

"Well, that *was* the plan, DJ. But for some reason it fell apart."

"That's because Grandmother thought you were pregnant."

"But that's just plain crazy."

"I know, Eliza. That's why I think we need to start over."

"But is your grandmother willing to talk to my mother? I mean, to convince her that I need to come back?"

DJ looked at her grandmother to see what looked like confused relief on her face. "Yes, I think she is."

"Well, Mother's not here right now, but she'll be back soon. How about if I tell her that Mrs. Carter will call around seven—does that work?"

DJ turned to Grandmother. "Can you call Mrs. Wilton at seven tonight?"

Grandmother simply nodded.

"She'll do it," DJ told Eliza.

"Oh, I hope this works, DJ!"

"Me too."

"Thanks!"

DJ hung up, then turned to Grandmother. "Eliza is *not* pregnant."

Grandmother sank down onto her chaise lounge and sighed. But then she looked at DJ with troubled eyes. "Then who is?"

DJ didn't say anything.

"Desiree?" There was a warning in Grandmother's voice.

DJ still kept her mouth shut.

"Oh, my goodness!" Grandmother's hand flew to her mouth. "It's not you, is it?"

DJ rolled her eyes. "No, of course not."

Grandmother leaned back and sighed. "Who then?"

"I can't say."

"But you know."

DJ nodded.

"I do appreciate your sense of loyalty, but I *will* get to the bottom of this." Grandmother frowned. "I know it's not Eliza or Rhiannon or you." She held up three fingers. "That leaves Kriti, Casey, and Taylor." Again she had a stricken look. "Oh, please, tell me it's *not* Taylor."

DJ pressed her lips together, then shook her head ever so slightly.

"Oh, I'm so glad that it's not. Poor Taylor. She's been through so much and she's been doing so well." Now Grandmother held up two fingers. "I certainly hope it's not Kriti. Her parents would be absolutely furious." She eyed DJ carefully.

Again DJ shook her head ever so slightly.

"So it's Casey." Grandmother made a sad *tsk-tsk* sound. "Well, that's not terribly surprising."

"Why do you say that?"

"Oh, it's not that I don't like Casey, but she's had such a chip on her shoulder for so much of the time. She was unhappy to come here and she has been so moody and difficult ... it just seems that she'd be the one to get into this kind of trouble."

"Please, don't tell her I told you."

"You didn't."

DJ nodded.

"Do her parents know?"

"No."

"She should tell them."

"I know. That's what I keep telling her."

"What about the father? Does he know?"

"It's Seth Keller. And he knows."

"Oh ... the Keller family." She made the *tsk-tsk* sound again. "They will not be pleased about this."

"Who would be?"

115

Grandmother made a forced smile. "Well, some families are more tolerant than others."

"Casey is worried her parents will be really upset."

"I'm sure they will be."

DJ was unsure how much to say, but since the cat was already out of the bag, she just plunged in. "Casey is considering an abortion."

Grandmother nodded sadly. "Yes, that doesn't surprise me."

"But her parents are really against that."

"And that doesn't surprise me either."

"So Casey is pretty confused."

"Understandably so."

"Taylor and I are the only ones who know. Well, and Seth."

"And how is Mr. Keller handling it?"

"Like a great big jerk." DJ filled her in on Seth, the breakup, and his taking someone else to the prom.

Grandmother's expression grew sour. "That's very unfortunate."

"And Casey's really depressed," DJ said. "I know she needs to talk to someone ... I mean, someone besides me. Someone who can help her to figure this thing out."

"Yes, you're right. She does need someone."

DJ felt hopeful. "Do you know anyone?"

"I'll give it some thought."

"And you won't be hard on her, will you?" Suddenly DJ was worried. "Casey is already really miserable."

"Yes, I'm sure she is. And, no, I won't be hard on her."

DJ leaned down to hug her grandmother. "Thank you!"

"I should thank you, DJ."

"And don't forget to call Mrs. Wilton," DJ said as she headed for the door. "Eliza is counting on you!"

Grandmother just nodded sadly. As DJ walked back to her room, she felt a little flicker of hope. Oh, she didn't know if Grandmother would really be able to talk sense into Mrs. Wilton, or if Grandmother would know who could help Casey, but it felt good to have someone else—an adult—involved in finding these answers.

**12**

*Last Dance*

"I have an idea for someone who could be my prom date," Casey announced from the backseat as DJ was driving to youth group.

DJ and Taylor exchanged glances.

"Who?" Rhiannon asked eagerly. She was in the backseat with Casey.

"Lane Harris."

"Hey, that's a great idea," Rhiannon told her. "I can't believe we didn't think of that already. Lane would already have his tux lined up and everything."

"Wait a minute." DJ turned down the road to the church. "We don't know for sure that Eliza's not coming back."

"I thought it was hopeless," Rhiannon said.

"Yeah," Casey agreed, "you said—"

"Something came up," DJ said quickly. "Grandmother is talking to Mrs. Wilton at seven."

"So you think there's a chance?" asked Rhiannon.

"I think so."

"That's great." Rhiannon said.

"Yeah, just great." Casey sounded deflated again.

119

"We'll still find you a date," Taylor called back.

"That's right," Rhiannon agreed. "There are lots of guys to choose from."

"Yippee," Casey said without even a slight glimmer of enthusiasm.

Soon they were in the youth hall. DJ had made sure to get them there early enough for some "social interaction." And she was pleased to see that Conner and Bradford were both talking to Emery. So it was the most natural thing in the world to go over and join them. Casey was the only one who didn't know Emery, and Conner introduced them.

"I can't believe you don't know Emery," Taylor said as she squeezed in between Emery and Conner. "Because he is entirely worth knowing."

Emery's cheeks were flushed. "Oh, I don't know about that."

"Emery was just telling us that he got accepted to Princeton." Conner directed this to Taylor. "You'll have to tell Harry that he's got another Princeton man to take his side in the ongoing battle of the universities."

Taylor laughed. "Yes, Emery, you should join us at the lunch table if you want to see a bunch of seniors acting like second graders."

"Thanks, but no thanks," he said.

The chatting and banter continued, and DJ actually thought they were all doing a pretty decent job of making Emery look good for Casey. Plus, Emery really seemed to be enjoying the attention. And when it was time to be seated, DJ had to ask herself—why hadn't they done this before? Not for Casey's sake, but for Emery's? Here was this really nice guy who happened to be uber-shy ... and with just a little encouragement, he was suddenly smiling and joking and having fun. Really, what had taken them so long?

Rod Michaels, the youth pastor, was talking about how God loved to give people second chances. He told the story of the disciple Peter and how he denied Jesus—not just once, or twice, but three times. And yet Jesus forgave him and Peter became one of the strongest Christian leaders of all time. "Sometimes we need to fall flat on our faces," Rod said finally, "to realize how much we need God. Because after we've tried everything and blown it and feel like total failures, we begin to understand how weak we are and how strong God is. Our perspective changes and we're ready to ask for help. Let's ask God for help now." Then he led them in a prayer, and it was all DJ could do not to nudge Casey with her elbow as in *hint-hint*. But she didn't.

As usual, they had refreshments and games afterward. Conner invited Emery to partner with him against DJ in a game of pool. So DJ grabbed Casey to be her partner. "I better warn you," Conner told Emery, "DJ is a shark, and I'm guessing Casey might be too."

"Oh, we'll take it easy on you," DJ assured them.

About midway through the game, DJ asked Conner if he had ordered his tux for the prom yet. Of course, she knew he'd already done it, but she pretended not to and he played along nicely.

"I can't believe it's on Saturday." DJ leaned down to take a shot, which she easily made. "It's going to be so fun." She stood, then looked at Casey. "Oh, I'm sorry, Case, I shouldn't be talking about—"

"Yeah, DJ," said Conner.

DJ went around the table for her next shot, then paused to talk to Emery. "Casey was invited to the prom," she explained quietly, "but her jerk of a boyfriend—"

"DJ," warned Conner, "just play pool, okay?"

121

"Yeah, right." DJ leaned over and took her shot, missing this time. She stood and tossed Casey a sympathetic look. "Sorry, it's just that I wish you—"

"Hey, why don't you go to the prom with me?" Emery said suddenly.

DJ knew that Conner had been coaching him on it, but she was impressed with how natural it seemed.

"I—uh—" Casey was tongue-tied.

"Sorry," Emery said quickly. "I guess that was socially stupid." His cheeks got flushed again. "I'm not very good at that—"

"No," Casey said quickly, "if you're serious, I'd like to go with you."

Emery looked honestly stunned. "Really?"

Casey nodded, smiling shyly. "Yeah."

"That's so great." DJ gave Emery a high five.

And Conner gave one to Casey. "We can all go together," Conner said. "Some of the other guys and I got a limo reserved. Emery, you just need to get your tux."

"Cool." Emery nodded, then leaned over to take his shot, which he made.

DJ wanted to break out in a happy dance, but for Casey's sake controlled herself. She didn't want to be too obvious.

Of course, by the time DJ was driving the girls home, Casey was questioning the whole idea. "I should've said no," she told them.

"Why?" Rhiannon questioned.

"Because I don't even know the guy," Casey said glumly.

"You'll get to know him," Taylor tossed back.

"But he's such a *church* guy," Casey argued. "And I am so not like that."

"You grew up like that," DJ reminded her.

"But I'm not like that anymore," Casey protested. "Really, we'll be like the weirdest couple at the prom."

"No you won't," Rhiannon argued.

"It's just all wrong," Casey persisted. "I should call him and cancel."

"That would hurt his feelings," DJ pointed out.

"But it's crazy!"

"Why?" Rhiannon demanded. "Why is it crazy?"

"Because he's such a *nice* guy!" Casey shouted.

"So?" Rhiannon shot back. "What's wrong with that? What's wrong with going to the prom with a *nice* guy?"

*"Because I'm pregnant."*

The only sound was the hum of the engine and soft whine of the tires on the road—no one said a word, and DJ was too stunned to even glance at Taylor.

*"What?"* Rhiannon's voice came out like a squeak.

Casey swore quietly.

"She said she's pregnant," Taylor said casually.

"That's what I thought she said." Rhiannon still sounded shocked. "Is it true?"

"Yes, it's true," snapped Casey. "And I think it's stupid for a pregnant girl to go to the prom with a nice church boy, don't you?"

Again, the car grew quiet.

"No ..." Rhiannon's voice was stronger now. "I don't think it's stupid."

"I don't either," said DJ.

"Me neither," added Taylor.

Casey let out an exasperated sigh, and that was the end of the conversation.

It wasn't until the next morning that DJ was able to ask her grandmother about the phone call to Eliza's mother. "How did it go?" she asked.

Grandmother's expression was hard to read. "I'm not sure."

"But you gave it your best shot."

"Yes, I did."

"But Mrs. Wilton didn't say whether or not Eliza was coming back?"

"She did not."

"Oh."

The other girls started to come in for breakfast, and DJ decided to let it go. She'd call Eliza later to see if she knew more. But when she called Eliza it went straight to messaging, and that didn't seem like a good sign. So when they got to school, DJ didn't see the point in trying to revive Eliza's prom queen campaign. Why get everyone's hopes up needlessly?

DJ tried to call Eliza again during lunch break, but with the same result—straight to messaging. This time DJ left a message. "Call me, Eliza, and tell me what's up. I know my grandmother talked to your mom, but did it do any good? Is there any chance you're coming back? I hope you're doing okay. Hang in there." She closed her phone and turned to Conner. "It's not looking very good for Eliza."

"Well, you've done all you can do to help, DJ. You've been a good friend."

"I wish I'd been a better friend early on."

He patted her back. "You can't change the past."

"I hope I get a chance to change the future."

Most of the talk at the lunch table was driven by the girls and focused on the prom. But DJ wasn't saying much. Mostly

124

she was ready for the whole prom queen thing to just be over with.

"I can't believe that everyone's predicting Madison will win," Daisy said sadly. "Now that Eliza's out of the race."

"Maybe we should campaign for Haley," suggested Kriti. "She's nicer than Madison."

"Depends on who you talk to," Casey told her. "I know girls who hate Haley."

"Maybe we should go ahead and vote for Eliza anyway," offered Taylor. "What could it hurt?" She nudged DJ. "Are you in?"

DJ shrugged. "Sure, why not."

"It'll be like a protest vote," Kriti told them.

"Yeah," said Daisy, "a protest over that stupid lowlife who made the MySpace page. I wish they'd catch her."

DJ didn't recognize the car in front of Carter House when she got home, but figured it must be one of her grandmother's friends. She was barely in the front door when she was practically tackled—by Eliza!

"What are you doing here?" DJ demanded.

"We just got here," Eliza told her as she grabbed Casey and Taylor and hugged them both.

"We?"

"My mother came with me." Eliza nodded toward the library. "We're having a meeting in there, and your grandmother wants you to join us, DJ."

"Sure." DJ followed Eliza to the library to find Grandmother and Mrs. Wilton sitting at opposite sides of the desk.

"You're just in time, DJ." Grandmother smiled. "Please, sit down, girls."

"How are you doing, Mrs. Wilton?" DJ asked as she took the seat next to her.

"As well as can be expected ... under the circumstances."

DJ nodded. "I understand."

"And I understand you were involved in Eliza's kidnapping and—"

"Involved?" DJ felt alarmed. "What do you—"

"I'm sorry, that came out wrong." Mrs. Wilton smiled slightly. "I meant to say you were involved in helping her. Eliza told me how grateful she was for your help, DJ. I want to express my gratitude too."

"Oh ... thank you."

"No. Thank you, DJ."

"Well, we're kind of like a family here." DJ glanced over to where Eliza was sitting nervously, literally on the edge of her chair. "And we've really missed Eliza."

Mrs. Wilton sighed. "Yes ... and Eliza has missed you."

"And we were really hoping she'd get to come back," DJ continued. "There's so much going on right now. Prom, the fashion show, graduation ..."

"Yes, I'm aware."

Grandmother cleared her throat. "Yes, we had really hoped to have Eliza with us until the end of the year." She smiled at Mrs. Wilton. "I had hoped that you would join us for the Mother's Day fashion show. It's a charity event and Dylan Marceau will be so disappointed to learn that he's lost one of his favorite models."

Mrs. Wilton frowned. "I really don't enjoy playing the heavy role, but you must understand my concern."

"As I said, I understand completely," Grandmother reassured her. "I can't apologize enough for not contacting you directly about the Palm Beach incident."

"But she tried," Eliza pleaded.

"After we got back to Crescent Cove, Eliza begged me to allow her to handle it." Grandmother folded her hands on the desk. "As you know, I try to treat the girls as adults … for the most part. I expect them to take responsibility for themselves."

"And I let her down," Eliza told her mother. "And I told you I'm sorry. And I told you that I just wanted to bury the whole thing. It seemed easier that way."

Mrs. Wilton looked upset. "Don't you realize how dangerous that was, Eliza? You could've been killed."

"I know, Mother." Eliza stood and began pacing. "But that wasn't really my fault. I mean, I got myself into it, but the guy was a creep."

"That's right," DJ agreed. "And he stalked Eliza without her knowing it."

"But I'll bet she'd know if it started to happen again," said Grandmother.

"Don't be too sure." Mrs. Wilton frowned.

"I know I'd be a lot more careful," Eliza shot back. "I did learn a thing or two, Mother."

"Yes, yes … I know you did."

"Here's what I think," DJ said suddenly. "I think something like that could've happened anywhere. In Louisville or Paris or even here in Crescent Cove. I mean, it's pretty hard to prevent someone from being evil. But Eliza is eighteen, Mrs. Wilton, and next year she'll be in college, and she'll be even more on her own than she is now. So you're going to have to let her go."

Mrs. Wilton nodded. "Yes, you're right." She looked over at Eliza. "I suppose I'm feeling a bit guilty."

"Guilty?" Grandmother looked surprised.

"For not being more involved in Eliza's last year of high school."

"But you and Daddy had your hands full with the vineyard and everything," Eliza said. "And I've really liked being here in Carter House. I've made some really good friends. And we've had some good times. I've actually learned a few things ... and I hope I'm growing up a little." She gave DJ a wistful smile. "But I know I have a long way to go."

Mrs. Wilton smiled ever so slightly. "Yes ... it's good you know that." She turned to DJ. "Is it true that you've been accepted to Yale?"

DJ glanced at Grandmother. Where was this going?

"Yes, it's true," Grandmother said proudly. "And she's been invited to visit their campus."

Mrs. Wilton turned back to DJ. "How about if I make a deal with you, DJ?"

"A deal?"

"Yes. I will allow Eliza to come back for prom and the fashion show ... and possibly until graduation ... if ..."

"If?"

"If you let Eliza go with you for the Yale visit."

"Can I even do that?" DJ looked to Grandmother, but her expression was blank.

"Of course you can," Mrs. Wilton assured her. "Eliza's father is already negotiating something with the dean of admissions. We suspect they may have declined Eliza's application simply to get us to up our donations. But I think if Eliza could go to visit there with you, DJ, you're just a normal sort of girl ... well, perhaps that would help Eliza to be seen in a different light."

DJ blinked. "Seriously?"

"Absolutely. Are you willing?"

DJ glanced over to see Eliza looking at her with big blue puppy-dog eyes. "Sure," DJ told Mrs. Wilton, "I don't see why not." She almost added that she didn't really plan on going to Yale, so even if Eliza made a bad impression, it wouldn't matter much. But, for Grandmother's sake, she didn't.

"Good." Mrs. Wilton smiled at DJ. "Now, if you girls will excuse us, Mrs. Carter and I need to discuss some more details."

"No problem." DJ was eager to get out of there.

Once they were out of the room, Eliza threw her arms around DJ in a tight hug. "Thank you, thank you, thank you!"

DJ hugged her back. "I'm glad you're back." She laughed as they stepped apart. "And there was a time when I never would've guessed I would say something like that."

"I know." Eliza grinned sheepishly. "I've been a spoiled brat for most of the year. And I've gone out of my way to make you miserable."

"Well . . ." DJ gave her a half smile.

"And I can't promise that I'll never go back to my old snooty-pants ways." She made a face. "The truth is I really *like* being a princess."

At least Eliza was being honest. DJ considered the whole princess thing. It had never appealed to her, but Eliza seemed to need it. "Maybe the problem isn't in being a princess — but in being a *selfish* princess. I don't think anyone would mind if you were a *nice* princess."

Eliza nodded. "That's exactly what I'm going to try to do."

And for Eliza's sake, DJ hoped that she'd succeed. After all, Eliza had mostly hurt herself when she played the role of entitled royalty. A spoiled princess stepped on toes and made enemies. Really, what was the point?

## 13
### Last Dance

ELIZA'S MOTHER JOINED THEM FOR DINNER that evening. And after Grandmother said grace, Eliza asked if she could say something.

"Certainly." Grandmother smiled at her.

Eliza stood. As usual, she was the picture of elegant perfection in what must've been a new and probably expensive outfit, possibly from Paris. Even DJ could appreciate the chic simplicity of the perfectly cut sleeveless linen top and sleek pants in complementary shades of pale blue, accented with delicate jewelry that probably was the real deal. Eliza really could pass for royalty. "I just want to thank everyone for working on my prom queen campaign while I was gone," Eliza began. "And I want to say that I don't deserve the kindness you have all shown to me. I know I've acted like a spoiled brat for most of this year, and I know I've hurt everyone at this table. For that I'm sorry. And I'm going to try to do better. I really am." She looked around the table. "Some of you might think I'm just saying this because my mother is here, but I'm saying it because I realize that I've been selfish and self-centered and, as DJ put it, 'a selfish princess.'"

Several people, including her mother, laughed at this.

"The truth is I *like* being a princess, but I'm going to try to take DJ's advice and be a *nice* princess. And for my first gesture as a nice princess, I've made all of you an appointment at Yo-bushi's Day Spa on Saturday—pedicures, manicures, facials, the works ... my treat. We'll *all* be princesses!"

After the girls expressed their gratitude, Grandmother cleared her throat. "That's very generous of you, Eliza, and I'm sure everyone appreciates it. But I hope you didn't forget that we have a short modeling practice on Saturday morning."

"I asked that all the appointments be scheduled for after eleven," Eliza told her.

"Perfect." Grandmother nodded to Clara to begin serving.

It seemed that all the girls were on their best behavior during dinner. Whether it was to impress Mrs. Wilton, or in gratitude of Eliza's spa gift, or simply that they were relieved to have Eliza back, DJ wasn't sure. But she could tell that Eliza's mother was impressed. Even Casey, who'd been grumpy all day, seemed to be trying to act normal.

"I must say," Mrs. Wilton declared as they were finishing dinner, "you are a lovely group of young ladies." She turned to Grandmother. "It seems you're doing a better job with your Carter House girls than I had thought."

DJ suppressed the urge to laugh. And, to be fair, maybe Grandmother had done a better job than DJ had thought too. Or maybe the girls were simply growing up. Or both.

"I have an announcement," Kriti said. "Daisy has asked for us to have an emergency campaign meeting for Eliza's prom queen campaign at seven thirty. We'll meet in the ballroom."

"Well, it's almost seven thirty now," Grandmother told them.

So they began to excuse themselves, and before long they were gathered in the ballroom, where Daisy took center stage.

"We all have to do everything we can for Eliza's campaign tomorrow," Daisy told them. "I've just heard that Haley's being dragged through the mud."

"How's that?" asked DJ.

"They're talking about her on MySpace, reminding everyone about when she tried to kill herself last fall, saying she's unstable now, and that she's got an eating disorder, and all kinds of other things."

"Isn't that slander?" Kriti asked.

"Not if it's true," Taylor told them. "It's only slander if it's false."

"Is it true?" Daisy asked. "Does anyone know?"

"Some of it's true," DJ admitted. "Not that it's a reason to publicize it on MySpace. Or a reason for Haley to lose votes."

"According to my sources, that's what's happening."

"Who are your sources?" DJ demanded.

Daisy looked slightly embarrassed.

"Come on," DJ urged her. "Who have you been talking to?"

Daisy made a weak smile. "My little sister is best friends with Madison's little sister—they're in middle school together."

"You're using your little sister as a spy?" Rhiannon asked.

"Not really. It's just that my little sister is really yappy," Daisy explained. "I mean, she just opens her mouth and everything comes flying out."

They laughed.

"So anyway," Daisy continued, "Madison is feeling really confident, and according to Lucy, my little sister, she is pulling out all the stops tomorrow. Lucy says Madison is going to win prom queen."

133

"Lucy says?" DJ made a face. "No offense, Daisy, but Lucy is in middle school ... how can she possibly know who's going to win?"

Daisy kind of shrugged. "I don't know ... but I just thought everyone should know."

"The point is," Eliza said, "I'm going to have to work hard to get votes tomorrow. And I appreciate any help you guys can give me. I had planned to have some really awesome giveaways for the last day, but because of, well, everything ... that's not happening." She pointed to a couple of grocery bags. "But I did grab these things this afternoon."

"What did you get?" DJ asked.

Eliza reached into the bag and pulled out some packages of candy. "Not very polished, but I thought it was better than nothing."

"Hey, a lot of kids will think it's perfect," DJ assured her.

Then Kriti and Daisy began scheduling the girls to manage the campaign tables before school and at noon. After that, the voting would begin.

"I just want to thank you all," Eliza said finally. "You have no idea how much your support means to me. And even if I don't win, I'll always remember that you girls were backing me. Thanks!"

On Friday morning, to help get things set up for Eliza, they all left for school earlier than usual. As she drove, DJ tried to ignore Casey's complaints from the backseat. "I don't see why we're all suddenly doing backflips for Eliza," she groused. "I mean, just because she's all goodness and light now. You can bet she'll return to her old spoiled self as soon as that crown's on her head."

"It's just one day," DJ told her. "Can't you let it go?"

"I just don't get why you're all being so —"

"We understand that you don't get it," Taylor told her. "But why don't you just chill, okay?"

Casey growled, but kept her mouth shut.

"That's better," DJ told her.

"Yes, little Miss Sunshine," Taylor teased, "if you can't say anything nice, don't say anything at all."

The girls went into school together and immediately began setting up Eliza's tables. Rhiannon arranged the colorful packages of candy, fanning them out to make a rainbow. Everyone had on an Eliza button and some of the girls were even wearing the pink Queen Eliza T-shirts. As students began to arrive, it was clear that they were surprised to see that Eliza was back in the running. Rumors had abounded that she was out of the race for good.

DJ smiled at Monica as she picked up a bag of M&Ms. "Eliza is back and she's strong. But she needs your vote."

"Don't forget to vote," Taylor told a guy who was pocketing a Snickers bar.

"The grocery store candy seems to be more popular than the fancy stuff," DJ said quietly.

"You know what they say." Taylor winked. "Ninety percent of the people have ten percent of the taste. And ten percent of the people have ninety percent of the taste."

DJ considered that. "I guess that puts me in the ninetieth percentile."

Taylor just laughed.

"Oh, oh." DJ nodded toward Madison, who was approaching. "Trouble this way comes."

"What are you guys doing?" Madison demanded.

"Campaigning." DJ gave her a big smile.

"But Eliza's out of the race."

"What made you think that?" Taylor asked.

"The fact that she left town and wasn't coming back."

"Well, she's baaa-ack," DJ said in a bad Schwarzenegger imitation.

"She might be back, but she's not on the ballot." Madison smiled smugly and walked away.

DJ and Taylor looked at each other.

"She's not on the ballot?" Taylor frowned. "How can that be?"

"I don't know." DJ stood. "But I'm going to find out."

Taylor nodded. "And I'll stay here and keep giving goodies to the kiddies."

DJ hurried down the hall to the table that Daisy and Eliza were manning and told them what Madison had just said.

"No way!" Daisy stood up and clenched her fists.

"That's what she said."

"But that's not fair," Eliza told them. "I never asked to be removed from the ballot. How can they take my name off just like that? I'm going to get to the bottom of this."

Eliza had a fair amount of people gathered around her table, so DJ told her to stay put. "I'll go to the office and try to find out what's going on. You keep campaigning."

"Thanks." Eliza gave her a bright princess smile.

DJ ran into Conner on her way to the office. "Hey, what's the hurry?" he asked. She quickly explained, and he offered to come with her. Soon they were standing in front of the vice principal's desk.

"Can we speak with you, Mr. Van Duyn?" DJ began.

"Two of my favorite students." He smiled. "Of course. Take a seat."

They sat down, and DJ quickly explained the situation, trying to give enough details without giving away too much.

"I was aware that Eliza Wilton's name had been removed from the ballot," he admitted.

"But why?" demanded DJ.

"It was brought to our attention that she has been truant."

DJ blinked. "Truant?"

"She has quite a number of unexcused absences."

"You mean this last week?" asked DJ.

"I couldn't say for sure."

"Well, that has to be it," DJ told him. "Because Eliza hasn't missed any school until now. And those should be excused."

"Apparently, they're not."

"But what if they were?" Conner asked.

"I'm afraid it's too late for that." Just as he said this, the first bell rang. "And speaking of late ..." He stood and smiled sadly. "I'm sorry I can't be of more help."

DJ and Conner both stood. DJ felt like screaming at the thick-headed vice principal, but she knew that wouldn't help. "Thanks anyway," she told him crisply.

"What now?" Conner asked as they left the office.

DJ thought for a moment. "I'll talk to Mrs. Seibert," she said. "You go ahead to class and I'll see what I can do."

Fortunately, Mrs. Seibert was much more reasonable. DJ had barely begun to explain the dilemma when Mrs. Seibert got the whole picture. "Of course Eliza will be excused. Under the circumstances, it's completely understandable."

"And her mother is here in Crescent Cove," DJ told her. "I'm sure she could write a letter."

"I'm not even sure that's necessary. A phone call should be sufficient." Mrs. Seibert looked puzzled. "In fact, I'm surprised that Eliza's absences even made it onto the radar ..." She paused to look out the one-way glass window, then chuckled.

DJ turned to see Tina Clark working the front desk. Her first class must be as an office assistant. That's when the light went on. "I get it!" DJ smacked her forehead. "Tina must've turned Eliza in."

"We don't know that for sure," Mrs. Seibert said. "But don't worry, Eliza's name *will* be on the ballot."

"Thank you!"

Mrs. Seibert smiled at DJ. "Eliza is lucky to have such a good friend."

DJ just shrugged. "I haven't always been such a good friend."

"Friendship is one of those things ... where there's always room for improvement." She handed DJ a slip of paper. "Here's your tardy excuse. You better scoot off to class."

DJ thought about what Mrs. Seibert had just said about friendship. It did seem to be true. It was like you could never really get being a friend down pat — probably because people were always changing. As a result, friendships changed too. In fact, it seemed that the friendships that didn't change, the ones that remained stagnant and old ... they were probably the most at risk of disintegrating.

## 14

### Last Dance

**DJ DECIDED TO KEEP HER SUSPICIONS TO HERSELF,** at least until they were sure Tina was the one who'd "ratted out" Eliza for truancy. And considering how tight the tensions about the prom queen race were getting, waiting was probably for the best.

"It's too bad that the election got so vicious," Rhiannon said at lunch. They'd been discussing the fact that someone had defaced a lot of Eliza's posters by drawing black mustaches, eyebrows, glasses, and spots on her photos.

"I agree," Eliza said. "In fact, I'm going to attempt a peace offering." She then stood up and walked over to the next table, where Madison and her friends were sitting. Suddenly the whole cafeteria got very quiet and it seemed that all eyes were on Eliza. Everyone probably expected to witness a hair-pulling catfight.

"Madison," Eliza said in a clear voice. "I know we've had our differences, but I just want to say that I harbor no ill feelings." Then Eliza stuck out her hand.

Madison was clearly caught off guard, but then she smiled in a catty way. "Very smooth, Eliza," she said loudly. "A last-minute attempt to get attention and gain a few votes." She shook Eliza's hand. "Unfortunately, I'm sure that most people will see through your little sham. We all know that you only care about one thing." She turned to her friends. "Isn't that right?" They laughed. "Your only goal is to have every single one of us bow down and kiss your feet." They laughed even louder. "Well, that ain't gonna happen!" And then her table cheered.

Eliza looked flustered. Without saying a word, she turned and walked out of the cafeteria. DJ felt sorry for her. But she knew that Eliza must've stepped into that knowing it could blow up in her face. And again, DJ wondered what made girls choose to campaign for things like prom queen. Oh, sure, DJ had been elected homecoming queen. But she'd had little to do with that crazy last-minute write-in campaign, and she'd been more shocked than anyone when she'd actually won—beating both Madison and Eliza. But to run for a queen's crown on purpose? Well, wasn't that sort of asking for trouble?

"Excuse me for being late," Grandmother said as she joined them at the breakfast table on Saturday. "I just had a phone call from Dylan Marceau. He called to say that DJ and Taylor's prom dresses should arrive here by noon."

"Well, that's a relief," Taylor said as she refilled her coffee cup. "I thought I was going to have to wear my new Jimmy Choos with my slip."

"I hope they'll fit properly," Grandmother said as she opened her napkin. "If not, perhaps Rhiannon could help out."

"That's cutting it pretty close," Eliza said.

"Knowing Dylan, the gowns will fit perfectly," Rhiannon assured them. "He has all your measurements."

"Unless someone has put on weight." DJ elbowed Taylor in a teasing way.

"Speak for yourself."

"Where is Casey?" asked Grandmother.

"In our room," Kriti said quietly.

"Is she unwell?" Grandmother asked.

"It was hard to tell." Kriti looked uncomfortable.

"Why is that?"

"She was still asleep."

"Oh ..." Grandmother looked around the table. "Now, girls, don't forget that we have modeling practice in fifteen minutes."

"And don't forget," Eliza reminded them, "we have to skedaddle over to Yobushi's by eleven. They worked really hard to schedule all six of us. And Mrs. Carter already said it was okay if we leave practice early to make it there."

"That's right," Grandmother agreed. "The other girls need more work than you do anyway."

"And we don't want to be late for practice," DJ reminded Taylor as they went upstairs. "Not after catching it last week."

"That's right," Taylor said in a mock serious tone. "Miss Walford might kick us out of the fashion show."

Eliza laughed from behind them. "Like that's going to happen."

"You never know," DJ shot back. And just to be on the safe side, DJ and Taylor both made a point to be on time. Of course, the other girls—Madison, Tina, Ariel, Jolene, Daisy, and Haley—must've come early. Because when the Carter House girls arrived, they were already there, gathered around Miss Walford and chattering away like groupies.

DJ and the other Carter House girls simply took their seats and waited. It seemed that Miss Walford was showing the girls her new necklace, and they were acting like it was an Olympic gold medal. She was eating it up. DJ actually wished that Grandmother would enter the room and loudly clear her throat. But then the little fan group broke up, and Miss Walford stepped onto the runway and clapped her hands. "Is everyone here?"

That's when DJ realized that Casey wasn't there yet. She was tempted to run and get her, but DJ didn't want to be late. Besides, Casey might be in a snit ... she might refuse to come.

"All right," Miss Walford said briskly, "let's get this thing started. Girls, please line up."

Taylor glanced at DJ with uncertainty as they stood and went over by the runway.

"Didn't you hear me?" Miss Walford was looking at Taylor and DJ. "I said line up."

Taylor started to go for the front of the line and DJ followed, but Miss Walford came down from the runway and stopped them. "Where are you two going?"

"To the front," Taylor said casually.

"Why?"

"Because that's how Dylan—"

"Is Dylan here?" demanded Miss Walford.

"No, but—"

"That's right. *No buts.*"

"Where do you want us to go?" Taylor asked crisply.

"Where were you last week?"

"Fine." Taylor glanced at DJ, and they both went to the end of the line.

"It's okay," DJ whispered. "Dylan will—"

"There will be no talking!" Miss Walford snapped. "Get ready, girls. On the count of three, I am turning on the music and we will begin."

DJ could tell that Taylor was seriously ticked at Miss Walford. For that matter, so was she. Not that there was much point in going to battle over this. DJ felt fairly certain that Dylan would iron out the wrinkles by next weekend. Or Grandmother would. As DJ took her turn on the catwalk, she wondered where Grandmother was and why she wasn't at least supervising the power-hungry Miss Walford.

The girls took directions, walking and moving and doing some crazy-looking poses that DJ felt certain Dylan and Grandmother would both hate. But the whole while she kept her mouth shut. Still, as they went through their paces, DJ could tell that Miss Walford was definitely showing favoritism to her dance team girls—her groupies. And DJ suspected that Madison and Tina had been telling her all kinds of stories about the Carter House girls and why they needed to be knocked down a peg or two, because it seemed Miss Walford was determined to do that.

"Good grief, Eliza," Miss Walford said. "Can't you walk in a straight line?"

Eliza looked like she was about to retaliate, but stopped herself. She simply continued walking in a line that was as straight as her mouth.

"DJ," snapped Miss Walford, "quit slouching."

"But I'm not even on—"

"Doesn't matter." She shook her finger at her. "Good posture is a must for everyone!"

And on it went until it was finally a quarter until eleven. DJ elbowed Eliza and nodded to the clock. "Yobushi's?" she whispered.

Eliza smiled in relief. "Thank goodness." Then she went over to speak to Miss Walford.

"Leaving *early*?" Miss Walford demanded. *"I don't think so."*

"I'm sorry," Eliza said politely, "but Mrs. Carter gave us permission. We all have appointments at Yobushi's and—"

Miss Walford's laughter cut her off. "As if that's even possible. Yobushi's taking six girls at once? You must think I was born yesterday."

"It *is* possible," Eliza told her. "And we have to leave *right now.*"

"That's right," Taylor said. "Eliza set the whole thing up for—"

"Anyone who leaves this room can forget about being in the Mother's Day fashion show," Miss Walford announced.

"Where's your grandmother?" hissed Eliza.

"I don't know." DJ frowned at the clock.

"It's *your* decision." Miss Walford put the music back on.

"No brainer," Taylor told the others as she led the way out. DJ followed, and the rest came scurrying along. On the second floor they met Grandmother coming out of Kriti and Casey's room.

"Is Casey okay?" DJ asked with concern.

Grandmother nodded, but her expression was somber.

"You guys head on over to the spa," DJ told Eliza. "I need to talk to Grandmother first."

"Okay," Eliza said. "See you there."

The four of them hurried down the stairs, and before DJ could tell Grandmother about Miss Walford's power trip, Grandmother was telling DJ about Casey. "I think I've convinced her to talk to her mother," Grandmother began. "But it will take a lot of encouragement from you and the other girls to keep her on track. The poor girl is very distraught over all this."

"I know. She's been really moody."

"Still … I think we had a good talk."

"Good."

"Now, you go in there and convince her to go to Yobushi's with you, DJ. I think that will be just what the doctor ordered."

"Okay, but—"

"Hurry, dear, you don't want to lose your appointment." Grandmother was already halfway to her room. "And have fun!"

"Thanks." DJ turned and knocked softly on Casey's door, then let herself in. She didn't know what to expect, but to her relief Casey was dressed and sitting in the window seat. "Are you ready to go?"

Casey shrugged.

"Come on, Case, it'll be fun," urged DJ.

"I don't know …"

"And have I got a story to tell you," DJ said mysteriously.

"What?" Casey looked intrigued.

"Let me grab my bag and I'll meet you downstairs. I'll tell you on the way to the spa."

As DJ drove to the other side of town, Casey listened, enthralled by DJ's story about Miss Walford's little power trip. DJ might've dramatized it a bit more than necessary, but only to bolster Casey's spirits.

"I'm almost sorry I missed that," Casey admitted.

"I doubt that it's over with yet," DJ told her. "It'll be interesting to see what happens when Dylan and Grandmother hear that the Carter House girls have been banned from the fashion show."

Casey actually laughed. "You know, DJ, your grandmother is okay."

DJ considered this. "Yeah, she is pretty cool for an old broad."

"We had a good talk ..."

"About?"

"About the baby."

DJ was surprised to hear Casey say it like that ... *the baby.* "Oh?"

"She told me that you're not the one who told her."

"Not in so many words," DJ admitted.

"She said Inez found my pregnancy test in Eliza and Kriti's trash can." Casey chuckled. "Guess that wasn't my most brilliant move."

"It worked out."

"Anyway, she was very understanding and wise."

DJ pondered that. *Wise* wasn't the usual word that DJ would choose to describe her grandmother, but it was sweet that Casey thought that.

"She told me I should tell my mom."

"And?"

"And I'm thinking about it."

"I know how much your parents love you, Casey. And, think about it, if my grandmother—a woman who is all about appearances—can be so understanding about your pregnancy, shouldn't your parents be even more so?"

"Maybe ..."

DJ parked in front of the spa. "Here we are," she said cheerfully. "Let the fun begin!"

Casey grimaced.

DJ reached over and put her hand on her arm. "Okay, Case, this is what I want you to do. It might not be the smartest thing. But as your friend, I'm asking you, okay?"

"What?"

"For just this one day, while we're at the spa, and while we're getting ready for the prom, and while we're at the prom ... could you just try to forget that you're pregnant?"

*"Forget?"*

DJ nodded. "Yeah. Give yourself a little break, okay?"

Casey looked unsure.

"Just for *one* day. And if you give yourself a break, you'll be giving the rest of us a break too. Do you get that?"

Casey nodded slowly. "Yeah ... I think I do."

DJ hugged her. "Thanks!"

As they went into the spa, DJ wasn't sure about what she'd just asked Casey to do. It wasn't like she wanted to pretend that being pregnant wasn't a big deal. But she just wanted Casey to cut herself some slack—and she knew that everyone else could use some too.

DUE TO THE STAGGERING OF APPOINTMENTS for six girls, they didn't get through with the spa until after two o'clock. But the entire time was slow paced and refreshing as they got facials and pedicures, soaked in the hot tub, had manicures, sat in the sunshine, enjoyed a nice lunch that Eliza had brought in, and eventually went home happy and relaxed.

"Thanks, Eliza," DJ said as they stood in front of the house. "I had no idea I'd enjoy it that much."

Everyone else chimed in, and Eliza seemed to appreciate their gratitude. "And don't forget that my mother is having appetizers sent over," Eliza reminded them, "and that they'll be set up at five for a little pre-prom soiree before the guys arrive." She turned and headed for her car.

"Where are you going?" Taylor called out.

Eliza patted her head. "To get coiffed. Anyone care to join me?"

They all passed, and Taylor announced she was going to take a nap. "All that hard work at the spa has exhausted me."

It seemed they all were worn out. Everyone slipped off to their rooms and for about an hour, the whole house was very quiet. When DJ woke up, she could hear the shower running and knew that Taylor probably was getting a head start on prom preparations. In an effort to split up bathroom time, DJ had taken her shower before her nap. But as she got out of bed, she noticed something. Two absolutely gorgeous dresses were hanging on the closet door. Someone must've brought them up while they were napping.

DJ ran straight to the pale aqua dress, holding it up to herself as she looked at the mirror. She was in astonishment. Although DJ didn't consider herself any kind of a fashion expert, and many would agree, she knew this dress was pure perfection. The top layer of fabric was so light and filmy that it seemed nearly weightless. And the way it seemed to catch and reflect the light in an iridescent way was magical. The cut was stunning and the fit appeared to be perfect. With a sweetheart neckline and a fitted low-waisted bodice, it was truly flattering. The skirt was full and flowing, but not too fluffy—perfect for dancing. Dylan had truly outdone himself. DJ knew she would feel like Cinderella tonight. And she could hardly wait!

"Can you believe it?" Taylor said as she emerged from the bathroom. "Inez brought them up while you were still asleep. She even steamed them for us."

DJ turned around, still holding the dress up in front of herself. "They're beautiful!"

"Dylan is a true artist."

"I can't wait to try it on."

"What are you waiting for?"

DJ looked at the clock. "It's only three thirty."

"Don't you want to be sure it fits?"

"Oh, yeah." DJ quickly tore off her sweats and soon had the dress on. "Oh, Taylor, look!" She spun around. "It's absolutely the best!"

Taylor had just taken her own dress from the hanger, but paused to stare. "Wow, DJ, that is superb. I think I'm jealous."

"Try yours!"

Soon they both had their dresses on, and while both dresses seemed totally perfect, DJ loved hers more. Fortunately, it seemed that Taylor loved hers more too.

"And they couldn't fit better," Taylor said as she carefully removed hers.

DJ continued to look in the mirror, turning from side to side. "How does Dylan do it?"

Taylor laughed. "Quit gawking at yourself. You still have your hair and makeup to—"

Her sentence was cut off by a scream—a truly bloodcurdling scream!

DJ grabbed Taylor's arm. *"Who is that?"*

"Sounds like someone's being murdered." Taylor grabbed her phone while DJ, still wearing her formal, ran out the door.

"Wait!" cried Taylor. "What if—"

The scream was coming from Rhiannon and Eliza's room. All of the girls and Grandmother merged in the hallway as DJ burst into the room to see what was wrong. There stood Eliza holding her icy blue prom dress, which was dripping in what appeared to be blood.

"Eliza?" cried DJ. "Are you hurt?"

Tears were streaming down Eliza's face.

"What is it?" demanded Grandmother. "What has happened?"

"Oh my—" gasped Casey.

"Have you been shot?" cried Kriti.

"No—no—I'm okay," Eliza sobbed. "Someone sabotaged my prom dress!" She held it out for them to see. "I think it's ... paint."

DJ reached out and touched and then smelled the fabric. "It's paint," she told them. "And it's nearly dry."

Eliza pointed to her closet, where the contents all seemed to be splattered in the same red paint. "It's all over everything," she sobbed, collapsing onto her bed.

"Who could've done this?" demanded Grandmother. She turned and looked at the girls. Everyone was there except Rhiannon. "Where is Rhiannon?"

"She's sewing upstairs." Eliza sat up and rubbed her eyes. "And she wouldn't have done this."

"Then who?" Grandmother asked sternly.

"Not any of the Carter House girls," Eliza said with confidence.

"Who then?"

"The other girls," DJ said suddenly. "They were all here when we left."

"The models?" Grandmother asked.

"Yes," Taylor agreed. "That must be it. Madison is the most likely suspect." She turned to Grandmother. "She was mad that Eliza came back in time to run for prom queen."

"Haley was here too," Eliza reminded them.

"I don't think Haley would do something like this," DJ said.

"I cannot believe anyone would do something like this." Grandmother was examining Eliza's closet. "This damage amounts to thousands of dollars. I believe that could be considered a felony."

"What's going on here?" asked Rhiannon as she came into the room carrying her gown. Then she saw Eliza's dress and let out a shriek. "What happened?"

They quickly explained, and Rhiannon was as indignant as the rest.

"We can't let them get away with this," Casey said.

"How can we prove they did it?" asked DJ.

"Maybe we should call the police," suggested Kriti.

"No ..." Eliza threw down her ruined dress. "Let's not."

"Why not?" demanded DJ.

Eliza's face was still wet with tears. "I just ... I just ... just can't."

DJ remembered what an ordeal it had been the last time they'd been with the police. "Okay ... I get it."

"So they just get away with it?" asked Kriti.

"Here's an even bigger question," said Rhiannon. "What is Eliza going to wear to the prom?"

Now they were all talking at once. Rhiannon rummaged through Eliza's paint-splattered closet only to find that all her formals were ruined.

"There's no time to shop for a dress," said Grandmother.

"You could borrow one of my old ones," offered Taylor, "but you'd have to get it altered since I'm bigger on top than you."

Eliza nodded. "I guess that would be okay. Thanks, Taylor."

DJ thought about how Taylor's style was usually pretty sophisticated and daring, whereas Eliza usually wore sweet delicate gowns with a definite fairy-tale princess sort of look to them.

"Most of my formals are darker colors." Taylor frowned. "And I don't think I have anything that I haven't already worn, but maybe no one will remember."

"Or maybe I could make some changes," offered Rhiannon.

DJ stepped up next to Eliza, holding the skirt of her gown out like she was about to curtsy. "So what do you think of this little number?" she asked.

"DJ," Grandmother reprimanded her. "Don't make Eliza feel worse."

"It's beautiful . . ." Eliza made a small half smile. "You look lovely, DJ. Like a princess."

"We're the same size," DJ reminded her.

Eliza looked confused.

"Why don't you wear it tonight?"

"Are you serious?" Eliza's blue eyes grew large.

"No, DJ," Taylor told her firmly. "Dylan designed it for you."

"And it's perfect on you, DJ," Rhiannon said quickly.

"That's very generous." Grandmother put her hand on DJ's shoulder. "But you don't have to do that, dear."

"I *want* to do it."

"No." Eliza shook her head. "I won't let you do that."

The room was quiet. DJ couldn't even explain where this was coming from—maybe it was a God thing—but she just really wanted to do this. And so she began to take off her dress. Standing there in her underwear, and not the pretty kind like Taylor and Eliza wore, she handed the dress to Eliza. "Please, just try it on. Do it for me." She smiled.

"DJ," pleaded Eliza, "I cannot take your dress."

"Please, just try it on."

154

Eliza slipped the dress on and Rhiannon helped with the zipper. Just as DJ suspected, it fit perfectly. DJ guided Eliza over to the full-length mirror. "You look beautiful, Eliza. And if you're crowned queen, you should be wearing it."

"But what about you?" Eliza was crying again.

"We'll fix her up," Rhiannon said quickly. She turned to Taylor. "Let me have a look at some of your dresses."

"And don't touch that closet," Grandmother commanded. "I want to take photos—just in case we find the culprit and need evidence."

"DJ." Eliza came over to stop DJ from leaving. "It's incredibly kind of you to offer your dress, but I really can't—"

"You have no choice," DJ told her. "You're wearing that dress."

"And if you know DJ," said Taylor, "you know it's useless to argue."

"I'm pretty sure she can take you," teased Casey.

"Lucky for you," Rhiannon told Eliza, "your shoes will look great with it."

"Now, everyone, it's getting late," Grandmother warned them. "I'm sure you still have a lot to do to be ready for your big night."

Rhiannon followed DJ and Taylor into their room. Taylor opened her closet and began to dig through it with Rhiannon. But it seemed that nothing they found was going to work. Meanwhile, DJ sat on her bed, still clad in just her underwear, and waited. Perhaps a teeny-tiny part of her regretted what she'd just done, but mostly she was just purely happy.

"What's that Bible verse about being a cheerful giver?" she asked.

"I can't remember the whole thing," Rhiannon called back, "but the gist is that God loves a cheerful giver."

"And that's how I feel about letting Eliza use that dress," DJ told them. "Cheerful."

"How about this one?" Taylor asked as she emerged with a silver-looking dress. "I've never worn it. In fact, I forgot I even had it."

"It's pretty," said Rhiannon. "The fabric is kind of like the one Dylan made. It's iridescent." She held it up to the light. "See how it changes colors, DJ?"

DJ got up to look at the dress. "It is pretty," she agreed. "How come you never wore it?" she asked Taylor. "Is something wrong with it?"

Taylor made a face. "It's a little too small on top."

Rhiannon brightened. "Bingo! Try it, DJ."

They helped DJ into it, and it fit fairly well, except that DJ was concerned about showing cleavage. "I don't know." Rhiannon squinted at the mirror, then pinched and pulled at the fabric, and finally promised she could have the dress fixed in about twenty minutes.

"But what about you?" DJ asked Rhiannon. "Am I taking away your primping time? What about your hair and makeup?"

"Look at her hair," Taylor said. "It's already perfect."

Rhiannon patted her naturally curly red hair and smiled. "Well, thank you. But I do plan to pin it up."

"I'll help you with your makeup," offered Taylor.

"Thanks!"

After Rhiannon left with the dress, DJ picked up her Jimmy Choos. "Do you think these will look okay with that dress?"

"Absolutely," Taylor assured her as she worked on her own hair. "And since Eliza's prom dress was light blue and yours was aqua, the guys' tuxes should be okay too."

"Almost like it was meant to be."

"Hey, underwear girl, why don't you plug in the hot rollers for your hair?" Taylor said.

"Why?"

"Because I'm going to do your do."

Before long all the girls were running in all directions, borrowing last-minute items, and asking for opinions. As DJ sat there in her underwear—nicer underwear now—and got her hair and makeup done, she thought how she would miss this after graduation.

"Here we go," announced Rhiannon as she burst into the room with Inez behind her, carrying the steamer. "First you try it on, and if it's right Inez will steam it."

"And while they're doing that," said Taylor, "I'll work on your makeup, Rhiannon."

Inez had a hard-to-read expression as she helped DJ into the dress. Taking her time to zip it in back, Inez said nothing and simply turned DJ around to face the mirror. DJ couldn't believe it was the same dress. "Rhiannon is a genius," DJ said as she admired the way Rhiannon had draped a piece of gauzy silvery fabric around the previously too-revealing neckline. She'd made a few other slight changes as well that made all the difference.

"Very pretty," Inez observed. "You want me to steam it now?"

"I can do it," offered DJ.

"No, you cannot." Inez unzipped the dress and carefully removed it.

"Are you mad at me?" DJ asked as she reached for her bathrobe. Somehow sitting around in her underwear with Inez did not feel right.

Inez was already steaming the dress. "Mad at you?"

"Yeah, you're acting weird."

Inez sniffed.

"Are you crying?" DJ went around to see Inez better. "Is something wrong?"

"I just think it's very kind of you to give your dress to Eliza." She looked up at DJ with watery dark eyes. "You are growing up to be a fine young woman. You make your grandmother proud."

"Wow . . ." DJ shook her head in amazement. "Thanks, Inez. Coming from you . . . well, that's very nice." DJ just stood and watched as Inez finished steaming the dress.

"There, how's that?" she asked.

"That looks great. Thanks." Then DJ hugged her. Inez acted like she didn't like it and waved her hand as if to push DJ away, but DJ saw her smiling as she left the room.

"Now for the moment of truth," DJ said to herself as she slipped the dress on again. She was surprised that steaming helped as much as it did; the smoothed-out fabric was suddenly incredibly reflective and luminescent. DJ slipped her freshly pedicured feet into the delicious Jimmy Choos, and for the second time that day, she really did feel like Cinderella.

"Oh, good," said Grandmother as she burst into the room. "You're here."

DJ turned to show her the dress. "Didn't Rhiannon do a good job?"

"She certainly did." Grandmother nodded in approval. "That girl has such talent. Someday we'll be saying we knew her when."

"I know it's not quite as exquisite as Dylan's gown, but then Rhiannon was a little short on time."

"I have something to add to your ensemble, if you don't mind."

"Sure." DJ waited. "What?"

"Turn away from the mirror."

DJ did as told and waited as Grandmother clasped something cool around her neck.

"Now look in the mirror."

"Wow!" DJ stared at the beautiful necklace. "Those look like real diamonds!"

"Those *are* real diamonds. And the setting is platinum."

"Oh, Grandmother, I can't possibly wear—"

"Yes, you can."

"But what if I lose—"

"I checked the clasp, it's secure. Besides, they're insured. Now hold out your hand." She dropped a pair of teardrop-shaped diamond earrings into DJ's palm. "I'll let you put these on." Grandmother waited as DJ fiddled with the earrings, then sighed in satisfaction. "Perfection."

DJ held out a shoe. "And it all seems to go with the Jimmy Choos that Dylan sent."

"Just like it was planned."

DJ smiled. "Maybe it's because God loves a cheerful giver."

"What's that?"

Just then Taylor, Rhiannon, Kriti, and Casey burst into the room, and suddenly they were all oohing and aahing over DJ's "thrown together" ensemble. No one noticed Grandmother quietly slip out the door.

"You guys look fantastic too," DJ told them as she admired the girls' dresses. Kriti was actually wearing an Indian sari that looked like spun gold. It had been her mother's, and Kriti looked like an Indian princess in it. Rhiannon's gown was varying shades of pale green with layers of fabric and ribbons and lace and beads—a real work of art. It seemed that each girl's dress represented her perfectly. And they all looked beautiful in their own unique way.

"Where's Eliza?" DJ asked.

"Downstairs with her mom," Kriti informed her. "She's afraid to see you."

*"Afraid?"*

"She's worried you'll look like something out of the ragbag and that you'll change your mind and demand your Marceau dress back."

DJ laughed. "Are you kidding? I feel like a million bucks."

"And look at this bling!" Taylor fingered the diamond necklace. "Looks like the real deal."

DJ grinned. "It is."

"Whoa," said Rhiannon. "Should we hire security guards or a Brinks truck?"

"Just don't tell anyone," DJ warned them.

When they got downstairs, Eliza was relieved to see that DJ didn't want her Marceau gown back. "Wow, DJ, who's your fairy godmother?"

"It takes a village of godmothers to dress Cinderella," Taylor joked.

Mrs. Wilton took DJ aside. "Eliza told me about what happened this afternoon."

DJ nodded. "We have our suspicions about who's responsible, but Eliza doesn't want to do anything about it."

Mrs. Wilton waved her hand in a dismissive way. "I agree with Eliza on this. There's no sense in inviting unwanted attention."

"I understand."

Mrs. Wilton reached for DJ's hand. "I just want to express how grateful I am for your generosity to Eliza." She glanced over to where Eliza was chatting with Grandmother. "You have no idea how much that means to her . . . and to me. Thank you very much."

"You're welcome," DJ said quietly. "But really, it all turned out fine. I mean, look at me. Rhiannon and Taylor put this together just like that." She snapped her fingers.

"Still, you didn't know they could do this. And I appreciate what you did."

Before long, the guys arrived. Photos were taken, appetizers were devoured, and then they were whisked away in a stretch limo. Tonight's catered dinner—without alcohol—was served at Lane's house, and this time his parents were present, although they stayed in another wing of the house.

Just before the group left, the parents came down and Lane did introductions. And when he got to DJ, he informed his parents that "this was the girl who was accepted at Yale."

Mr. Harris firmly shook DJ's hand. "Good for you. You couldn't have chosen a better school."

"Except she's not sure she's going," Lane said in what sounded like a challenge.

"Not going?" Mr. Harris looked stunned. "Why not?"

"I haven't actually decided. I was a late applicant at Yale . . . in the meantime I was accepted at Wesleyan U." DJ reached for Conner's hand, grasping it and giving it a squeeze.

"Fine for a small school, I'm sure," Mr. Harris said, "but not Yale."

"DJ and I are going to do a day trip to campus next week," Eliza told him. "So DJ can check it out and hopefully make up her mind."

"Excellent plan," Mr. Harris said. "You should take Lane for a guide. He knows his way around that campus."

"I consider myself invited," Lane told them. "And I'll show you why Yale is the best university on the planet."

And so as they rode to the prom, the great debate about college ensued again. DJ continued to hold onto Conner's hand. She respected that he didn't engage and that, when provoked or put down, he didn't respond defensively. In fact, he was even able to make some pretty good jokes about the Ivy Leaguers without offending anyone. DJ appreciated that about Conner. He was one of those rare guys with both feet on the ground. And that was just one of the reasons DJ didn't want to let him go. Did that mean she'd follow him to Wesleyan? She wasn't sure. And as the rest of them argued about schools, DJ realized that this was a decision she'd need to place in God's hands.

**16**

*Last Dance*

DJ KNEW THAT THE BEST PLACE TO FIND CATTY GIRLS on prom night (and who would want to?) was in the ladies' room. But that wasn't why she went there. She wanted to make a quick adjustment to her bra, which for some reason kept slipping around while she was dancing. And being a confident girl, she didn't drag any of her friends off the dance floor to go with her either. So she was in the stall with her dress half off, tightening the back of her bra, when she heard a bunch of noisy girls come in. She knew right off that it was Madison and her followers, and for that reason she moved to the far corner of the stall and remained still.

"Eliza thinks she's going to be prom queen," one of the girls said. It sounded like Jolene. "You can tell by the way she's acting. All smug and superior."

"She always acts like that," Madison said lightly. "All the Carter House girls belong to the same stuck-up snot club."

"Where do you think Eliza got that dress?" Tina's voice sounded suspicious. "Everyone's talking about how great she looks."

"I heard someone at the punch table say it's a Dylan Marceau original," Jolene told them.

"We knew that Taylor and DJ were supposed to wear Marceau dresses tonight," Madison said.

"Maybe he made one for Eliza too," Tina suggested.

"Then why wasn't it in her room?" Madison seethed.

"Maybe she hid it in one of her friends' closets," Jolene said.

"I should've hit all their closets while I had the chance." Madison's voice was quiet but mean.

Tina laughed. "It would've been funny to see if they all could've come up with a last-minute gown."

DJ burst out of the stall. Her dress was still half off-half on, but she didn't care. "You guys totally stepped over the line today." She kept her voice calm as she slipped her arms into her dress and then pulled it up, reaching awkwardly behind her to zip up the back. "You went too far."

The three girls stared at her as if she were an apparition. Then Madison seemed to recover. "What do you mean, DJ?" she asked in a saccharine voice. "What are you talking about?"

DJ looked into the mirror, watching the three girls' reflections off to her side as she continued to adjust her dress. She smoothed down the gauzy fabric, then checked to make sure her diamonds were still intact. "You know exactly what I mean," she said coolly. She turned and looked Madison right in the eyes. "Eliza is wearing *my* dress tonight. Because you ruined hers. And not only her prom dress, but her entire wardrobe."

"Eliza's whole wardrobe is ruined?" Tina asked with what seemed genuine curiosity.

"Says DJ," Madison retorted.

"And FYI, girls, Eliza's wardrobe was worth thousands of dollars—which might make your little vandalism act fall into the felony category."

Madison looked slightly surprised, but said nothing.

"And you may be interested to know that my grandmother is not a bit pleased about it."

"What *are* you talking about?" Madison put on her best innocent face and her fidgeting friends attempted to imitate her. "How can I possibly be responsible for ruining Eliza's wardrobe? This is ridiculous."

"Don't play stupid." DJ reached into her little beaded bag, one that Rhiannon had loaned her from her retro collection, and retrieved her lip gloss, taking her time to apply it and blot it with a paper towel. Then she dropped the lip gloss back into the bag and pulled out her cell phone and held it up. "It's all right here."

"What?" demanded Madison.

"The little confession you just made." DJ knew she was stretching things a bit, but Madison didn't know that. The truth was it was all right there in her head. If they wanted to think she'd taped their conversation on her phone, let them.

Madison stepped toward DJ. "Why don't you just hand that over to me," she said quietly. Her eyes looked serious.

DJ closed the phone and considered dropping it back into her bag, but worried they might grab the bag and run. So she dropped her phone down the bodice of her dress.

"Clever," Madison said in a chilly tone. "Jolene, you go block the door so no one can come in here."

DJ feigned a laugh. "Seriously, what are you going to do, Madison? Do you plan on mugging me in the ladies' restroom with all our friends within shouting distance?"

"Madison?" Tina's voice sounded concerned. "We should just go."

Madison continued to approach DJ with a menacing expression.

"Madison," DJ warned her, "you do know that I'm an athletic girl, don't you? I mean, I work out, I do sports . . . and you don't. Are you sure you want to try to take me? I'd hate to hurt you."

"Madison!" Tina's voice was louder. "What are you doing?"

"I want that phone!"

DJ looked at Tina. "I think Madison is losing it, Tina. Maybe you should get her out of here and see if you can get her some professional help."

"Give me that phone, DJ!"

DJ stood straighter now. "If you girls will excuse me, I'm sure my friends are missing me by now." She locked eyes with Madison as she began to walk toward her. DJ was prepared to be tackled, but she felt confident she could hold her own, and if all else failed she would simply scream for help.

"Let us in," came girls' voices from where Jolene was attempting to barricade the door. "Quit blocking the door!"

Suddenly several girls, including Daisy and Monica, burst into the bathroom. "What's the matter with you, Jolene?" Madison asked.

"Hey, DJ." Daisy glanced around curiously. "What's going on here anyway?"

"Madison was just threatening to steal my cell phone," DJ announced loudly enough for everyone to hear.

"Huh?" Daisy looked confused.

"Come on, Madison," Tina urged. "Let's go."

Daisy walked over to DJ. "Seriously?"

"I overheard them talking about something they aren't very proud of," DJ said. "But, don't worry, it's under control."

"Are you sure?" Daisy looked concerned. "It looked like they were trying to take you out—three against one?"

DJ chuckled. "I'll let you know if I need help."

"Yeah, between you and me, we could take 'em." Daisy grinned.

DJ hoped it wouldn't come to that. But at the same time, she really did not want to see Madison get away with this. Despite Mrs. Wilton and Eliza's desire to keep the vandalism under wraps, it seemed that Madison needed some kind of consequence.

"Hey, what took you so long?" Conner asked when she rejoined him.

"Can you keep a secret?"

His eyes lit up. "Sure. What is it?"

She led him back to a quiet corner and told him the whole story. "Can you believe that?"

"No way!"

She shook her head in unbelief. "I know. It sounds like I'm making it up. But it's all true."

"Want me to hold onto your cell phone for you?"

She chuckled. "Well, it really doesn't have their conversation on it."

"But they don't know that."

"Okay." She turned toward the wall and fished the phone out of her dress, then turned back and handed it to him. "Thanks."

"It's still warm." He grinned.

"So ... anyway, I'm kind of stymied."

"If Eliza and her mother don't want the police involved, it doesn't seem like there's much you can do. Well, besides making them uncomfortable."

DJ nodded. "And that's worth something."

"Eliza seems to be having a great time tonight." Conner nodded toward the dance floor where Eliza and Lane were dancing. "It was cool that you let her wear your dress, DJ." He turned and looked back at her. "But if you'd told me you were wearing the designer original and Eliza's dress was from Target, I wouldn't have known the difference. The truth is, I think you're the most beautiful girl here."

She laughed. "Thanks. Now let's get back out there and I'll see how uncomfortable I can make Madison. I want to see her squirm."

"What if she wins tonight?" he asked as they walked toward the dance floor. "Would you say anything?"

DJ frowned. "What would I say?"

"I don't know . . ."

"You and me both."

DJ noticed Casey and Emery out on the dance floor again. Casey was actually laughing and smiling. It seemed that for one evening, she had forgotten about her condition. Or else she was putting on a good show for Emery's benefit. Either way, DJ was happy for her.

When it came time for the coronation, thankfully Madison did not win the crown. But neither did Eliza. It was Haley who was honored as prom queen. Although DJ felt sorry for Eliza, she was happy for Haley. And to everyone's surprise, as they drove home, Eliza confessed that she didn't mind losing that much.

"Oh, I'll admit it stung a little at first," she told them. "But then I thought about all my friends—I mean you guys—and I thought about how much we've been through this year and how patient you've all been with me and how you all campaigned for me even when I was in Louisville having a breakdown." She chuckled. "And I remembered all the times I've acted like a spoiled brat, and I just thought to myself, I've already won something a lot better than a prom queen crown."

They all clapped and cheered.

"Thank you." Eliza held up the smaller coronet that had been awarded to the second-place winner. "Besides, I'm still a princess!"

"At least you beat Madison," Casey said.

DJ was bursting to reveal what she'd overheard in the restroom, but knew Eliza wouldn't appreciate her closet ordeal being made public. And, really, it could wait. Besides, DJ wished she could come up with some kind of plan that would bring justice for everyone—quietly. There had to be a way to make Madison pay restitution for what she'd done. DJ decided to talk to Grandmother about it tomorrow.

17

last dance

"I'M NOT SURE THERE'S VERY MUCH WE CAN DO, DJ,"
Grandmother told her Sunday afternoon. DJ had just replayed
the prom restroom scene and Grandmother was still shaking
her head in amazement.

"You mean because Mrs. Wilton and Eliza want it kept
quiet?"

"Yes. Although I will certainly give Miss Dormont her
walking papers when it comes to the fashion show." She made
a *tsk-tsk* sound. "Other than that, it feels that my hands are
tied. You don't have any actual evidence. Even if you did, we
can't get the law involved."

"But I wish there was a way to make Madison suffer a
little." DJ was pacing in Grandmother's suite. "It seems like
she should at least learn a lesson. It's not like this is the first
time she's gotten away with something either. We're pretty
sure she's the one who slandered Eliza online, but we can't
prove it. Anyway, she just needs a little wake-up call."

"Being excluded from the fashion show is—"

"Something more than that." DJ sat down and looked at Grandmother. "Shouldn't she have to pay for her crime? Do public service or something?"

"The Wiltons won't be interested in any restitution ... if that's what you mean."

"Maybe Madison should be forced to donate the amount of what she destroyed to charity? Don't the fashion show proceeds go to the Boys and Girls Clubs?"

"Yes ..." Grandmother grew thoughtful. "I know they'd happily take any donations. But I'm not sure that Madison could afford the value of Eliza's clothes. Out of curiosity, I did a quick inventory when I shot the photos. The total was rather staggering."

"I can imagine." DJ stood. "What if we got Eliza to agree to confront Madison, out of court ... privately ... and demand that Madison donate the amount of damage to the Boys and Girls Clubs—either in money or in *volunteer* work?"

Grandmother smiled. "Why, DJ, that's an excellent idea."

"And it might do Madison some good to see how other people struggle," DJ continued. "It might remind her that she's got it pretty good even if she didn't get crowned prom queen."

Grandmother was writing something down. "Now, DJ, you don't need to get into the middle of this little skirmish. I'll speak to my attorney and Mrs. Wilton and I'll handle the situation from here. The less involved you can be, the better it will probably go. And if I need you as a witness, I'll let you know."

"But you'll let me know how it's going?" DJ asked as she was leaving.

"If and when there is news, I will keep you apprised. But it may take some time. After all, this is a busy week with the fashion show preparations and all. But in due time, DJ, Madison will get her comeuppance."

As she went downstairs, DJ hoped that she wasn't being vengeful. It's not like she wanted to punish Madison just to see her hurt. But she did want Madison to take responsibility for her actions. And maybe even to learn from her mistakes. What was wrong with that? Just the same, DJ was relieved to hand it over to Grandmother.

"Don't you think you should tell the others?" Taylor asked DJ as they got ready for school on Monday morning. DJ had just disclosed the prom night bathroom incident without really meaning to, probably because she felt nervous about Madison and her friends.

"Why?" DJ did one last swipe of mascara.

"In case Madison has mafia ties and she's put a hit on you?" Taylor's words were sarcastic, but her eyes showed concern.

DJ laughed. "Yeah, right."

"Well, the idea of Jolene barricading the door of the bathroom is a little creepy, don't you think?"

DJ nodded. "Yeah, I'll admit I was a little worried. I mean, I thought I had a good chance of getting out alive, but I didn't want to ruin your dress."

Taylor tossed her makeup sponge at DJ. "Okay, let's just get serious for a moment. Madison knows that you know. You are like a witness. What if she attempts some crazy stunt to keep you from talking?"

"I already talked."

"Yes, I know. But Madison isn't the brightest porch light on the street. And besides that, she's just plain mean."

"Seriously, Taylor, what do you think she'd do?"

"Pay someone to beat you up when no one's looking."

DJ considered this. "Oh."

"Or she might go after one of the other girls. You said it yourself, it sounds like she hates all of us."

DJ frowned. "I just don't understand how a person can be so filled with hate and have much of a life."

"That's her problem ... Madison needs to get a life."

"And she needs God."

But Taylor had convinced DJ. When Grandmother excused herself early from the breakfast table to meet with Eliza's mother, who had offered to help with the fashion show during her remaining week in Crescent Cove, DJ told the rest of the girls about Madison.

"I can't believe you didn't tell us during prom," Casey said in an offended way.

"Because I didn't want to ruin things," DJ told her.

"So why are you telling us now?" Eliza sounded slightly irritated.

"Because I told her to," Taylor admitted. "We all know Madison is a loose cannon, and she seems to hate us all equally. Think about it. If she had no concerns about locking DJ in the bathroom and using force to take her cell phone—at the prom—what else do you think she might do?"

"Or get someone to do for her," DJ added.

"Plus, she's probably still mad that she didn't win prom queen," Kriti pointed out.

"But I didn't take that from her," Eliza protested.

"That's not all," DJ said. "Grandmother knows about all this and she's removing Madison from the fashion show this week."

"So Madison won't be a very happy camper." Taylor refilled her coffee.

"I feel kind of sorry for her," Rhiannon said.

"I sort of do too," DJ admitted. "I mean, I don't like what she's done, but I do feel sorry for her. It's so desperate and pathetic ... like she's on a path to self-destruct."

"I don't feel sorry for her," Kriti said firmly. "She's *evil*."

"I agree." Casey pounded her fist on the table. "And if she comes after me, I'll be ready."

"How?" Taylor asked her.

Casey shrugged. "I don't know. But I'll be looking over my shoulder this week."

"Speaking of this week," Eliza directed this to DJ. "Why don't we drive over to New Haven in the next few days?"

"To check out Yale?" asked Taylor. "Or to play hooky?"

"Both," Eliza told her slyly.

"I guess we could do that." DJ reached for her second blueberry muffin, thankful that Grandmother wasn't around to frown at her caloric consumption.

"I can drive if you want," Eliza offered. "And Lane can be our guide."

DJ thought about her unfortunate ordeal with Madison and the possible repercussions, and figured one day out of harm's way might be a nice little break. "How about tomorrow or Wednesday?"

"Great. I'll check with Lane and we'll nail it at lunchtime. We'll need to get excused from school." Eliza frowned. "And I'll need to go shopping."

"Shopping?" DJ looked confused.

"Ninety percent of my clothes are toast, remember?"

"Oh, yeah."

"Plus, I'll need something *extra cool* to wear on campus."

"Right . . ."


"Have you seen Casey?" Taylor asked DJ in an urgent voice when they met in the cafeteria.

"No. What's up?"

"She must've made Madison's hit list."

"What? Why? Is she okay?" DJ remembered Casey's words about being ready to take Madison on. What if it had really happened?

"Apparently Seth got drunk on prom night and spilled the beans to Jolene that Casey is pregnant."

"And Jolene told Madison."

"And now Madison is telling everyone. She's ecstatic that one of the Carter House girls is pregnant." Taylor scowled. "If Madison had more brains, she could've used it as blackmail to keep the heat off of her."

"Do you think Casey knows?"

"That's my guess. She wasn't in my economics class."

DJ pulled out her phone and hit speed dial. After a couple of rings, Casey answered in a dejected tone. "Hi, DJ."

"Case? Are you okay?"

"How do you define okay?"

"I heard what happened."

"Yeah . . . I guess I should've known it would slip out. But I didn't think it would come from Seth."

"Taylor said he was drunk."

"Figures."

"So where are you?"

Casey sighed loudly. "Sitting in the town park with the pigeons and other losers."

"Oh, Casey, you're not a loser."

"I just can't—can't do this, DJ." Casey's voice broke.

"Do what?"

"I can't *face* everyone—not with them knowing. I can't come back to school."

"But what'll you do?"

"I don't—don't know." She sniffed loudly.

"How can I help you, Casey?"

"You can't." There was a pause. "It's like I almost . . . almost made myself believe it wasn't true. This past weekend I pretended I wasn't pregnant, and it seemed real. And then I came to school and reality slapped me across the face." Now she was crying really hard.

"I'm coming to get you," DJ said. "Stay where you are." DJ closed her phone and turned to Taylor. "She sounds desperate."

"Do you want me to come?"

"I don't think so. But could you go talk to Mrs. Seibert? Go ahead and tell her what's going on. We can trust her. And she might have some advice."

DJ met Conner on her way out. "Hey, where's the fire?" he said.

"Ask Taylor to fill you in," she said quickly. "And pray for Casey."

He nodded and DJ ran toward the parking lot. She drove straight to the park, but when she looked around she didn't see

Casey. Finally she spotted her sitting on the ground beneath a tree with her head tucked into her knees. DJ ran over and threw her arms around her. "Casey, it's going to be okay."

"How can it be okay?" Casey looked up with a tear-streaked face. "My life is over."

"No, it's not. Lots of girls have lived through—"

"I'm not lots of girls." Casey stood with a defiant expression. "And I know what I have to do."

"Call your mom?"

She shook her head and began walking away. "No. My parents are not going to find out about this because it's over with."

DJ walked with her. "Meaning?"

"I'm ending this pregnancy."

"But Casey . . ." DJ reached out to stop her from walking.

"It's my life, DJ. My choice."

"But are you making this choice because it's what *you* want? Or are you making it because of Madison's interference?"

"I'm not strong enough to do this."

"You have friends, Case, and family."

"You offered to help me, right?"

"Of course."

"Then drive me to the women's clinic."

DJ bit her lip.

"If you don't drive me, I'll just walk."

"I'll drive you on one condition."

"What?"

"That you let me call my grandmother."

"Your grandmother already knows what's up."

"She knows you're pregnant. She does not know you're on your way to get an abortion."

"Fine," Casey snapped. "Call her."

While DJ called Grandmother, quickly giving her this news, Casey called the women's clinic and asked if she could come in. They both hung up simultaneously.

"Ready?" Casey asked with a hard look in her eyes.

"I guess." DJ walked slowly back to her car. She had no idea what, if anything, Grandmother could do to help, but at least she knew.

"Can you move any slower?" Casey asked as DJ dug through her bag for her car keys.

"I'm sorry," DJ said indignantly. "I guess this is a little upsetting."

"Tell me about it."

Of course, the truth was, DJ was trying to stall. And when she took the wrong street to the clinic, Casey pointed it out.

"Sorry ... I feel like I'm in a fog."

"Whatever ..." Casey fidgeted in the passenger seat. "And you don't have to stay with me when we get there."

"Right ..." DJ shook her head. "I'll just dump you there, leave you by yourself, and go back to school."

"Whatever."

Finally they were at the women's clinic. Thankfully, the receptionist wasn't moving any faster than DJ had been. It took her several minutes to find the paperwork Casey had completed during her last visit.

"Lucky for you it's a slow day. If you're willing to wait, the doctor can see you in about an hour or so."

"An hour or so?" Casey let out an exasperated sigh.

"Unless you'd rather make an appointment for another day." The receptionist smiled. "Then you wouldn't have to wait."

"No thanks. I'd rather wait." Casey turned and marched over to the waiting area and picked up a ratty-looking magazine and began flipping through it.

DJ followed her, thanking God for this short reprieve and praying for a miracle. They'd only been there about ten minutes when DJ's phone rang. She stood to answer it, slowly moving outside when she heard her grandmother's excited voice on the phone. Grandmother wanted to know what was happening and whether or not Casey was "undergoing treatment" yet.

DJ explained the hour-long wait. "But Casey seems determined."

"I just called Casey's mother and told her what was going on," Grandmother said. "Naturally she was extremely agitated and very concerned."

"And?"

"And she wanted to call Casey and tell her not to do this."

"So is she going to?"

"She's worried that she and Casey might get into a fight and that Casey will proceed with the abortion just to show her she can."

DJ thought for a moment. "That sounds about right."

"So Mrs. Atwood asked if we would do what we can to dissuade Casey while she attempts to book a flight."

"She's coming here?"

"Yes."

DJ sighed. "Good."

"You say Casey has an hour-long wait?"

"Around that."

"I'm leaving the house now."

"To come here?"

"Of course."

Relief washed over DJ as she thanked her grandmother and hung up. She looked up at the clear blue sky and the few puffy white clouds floating overhead, and wondered why anyone would want to extinguish the life of anything. Then she asked God to do a miracle and to prevent Casey from going through with the abortion.

**18**

*LAST DANCE*

WHEN DJ RETURNED TO THE WAITING area, SHE somehow knew that she needed to keep the news about Casey's mother to herself.

"Who was on the phone?" Casey asked.

"My grandmother."

"Oh . . ."

"She wanted to know if you were, uh, being treated or not. I told her we had to wait."

Casey tossed the magazine back onto the pile and looked at her watch. "This is going to be a very long hour."

"Anyway, Grandmother is coming over."

"Here?" Casey looked alarmed.

"Yes."

"Did you tell her to come?"

"No, of course not. She's coming because she wants to. She cares about you, Casey."

"I don't want her to come." Casey looked anxious. "Call her back and tell her not to come."

"It's too late. She said she's on her way."

Casey glanced around the waiting area, reminding DJ of a trapped animal. "But why is she coming? There's nothing she can say or do to stop this. It's not like I need parental consent or anything."

"I know." DJ put her hand on Casey's shoulder. "She's just coming because she wants to."

Casey grabbed up another magazine, flipping frantically through it without appearing to even look. DJ leaned back, closed her eyes, and silently prayed. After about ten minutes, Grandmother arrived. She sat next to Casey, looking out of place in the shabby waiting area in her pale green silk pant-suit, flowing silk scarf, and perfectly styled gray hair. But she didn't seem to notice as she took Casey's hand and began to talk.

"Now, I know you're not going to be pleased to hear this, but I spoke with your mother, Casey, and she's getting a flight out here. If not today, tomorrow."

"What? You called my mother?" Casey's voice was loud enough to draw the attention of the receptionist, who came over to see if there was a problem.

"I am Casey's guardian," Grandmother informed her.

"Casey doesn't need permission for this procedure," the receptionist said a bit brusquely.

"I am aware of that. I only came to ask her to postpone this appointment until her mother arrives from California."

"Oh …" The receptionist looked around. "Maybe you should use one of the counseling rooms to talk privately."

Grandmother thanked her and the three of them were soon sitting in a small room, but it was Grandmother who did the talking. Casey and DJ listened.

"I'm going to tell you both a story that no one else knows," Grandmother began. "Or rather a confession." She looked at

Casey. "I was exactly where you are once. I was unmarried and pregnant, and I thought the only way out was to get an abortion, which wasn't even legal at the time. But that's how desperate I was."

DJ tried not to look as shocked as she felt.

"In my industry, back in the fifties, unwed pregnancies were even less acceptable than nowadays. To me the only way out seemed to be to get rid of the baby and get on with my life."

"So did you?" asked Casey.

"No." Grandmother looked at DJ. "The baby was Desiree's mother, Elizabeth." Her face softened as she continued. "But it wasn't easy ... and it was a blow to my pride ... but I never regretted it. Not for a minute." She smiled at DJ. "I still don't. It was my mother who encouraged me to keep the baby. She wanted to help raise Elizabeth and I let her. I suppose I do regret that."

"You mean you regret keeping the baby?" asked DJ. "Instead of giving her up for adoption?"

"No ... no." Grandmother shook her head. "I regret allowing my mother to raise Elizabeth. I wish I'd done that myself. But I was young and headstrong and my career was all I cared about." She turned to Casey. "I'm not suggesting you'll want to keep and raise your child, Casey, I'm just saying I don't believe you'll regret talking to your mother about it before you make your final decision."

"Please, talk to your mother first," DJ urged her.

Casey was crying again.

Grandmother reached over and put her hand on Casey's. "We respect that this is your decision, Casey, but if you make it too hastily ... you could be sorry. And then it will be too late. What can it hurt to wait a week or so?"

DJ handed Casey a tissue box, waiting as Casey loudly blew her nose.

"I guess I can postpone my appointment for a week."

Casey stayed home from school on Tuesday, and in the afternoon DJ drove her to the airport to pick up her mother. Casey fidgeted and fretted all the way there, but once Mrs. Atwood embraced her daughter in a long, tight hug, it seemed that Casey's anxiety slowly melted away. DJ listened as they talked during the trip back home. She could tell Casey's mom was treading carefully, trying to be understanding and supportive. And Casey steadily warmed up until DJ began to feel that hope was in sight.

"I think you should come home with me," Mrs. Atwood told Casey as DJ pulled up to the house.

"What about school?"

"You can finish up at your old high school."

"But graduation is only a few weeks away."

Suddenly they were arguing, and DJ made a quick exit from the car, hoping they could iron this one out themselves. She understood Casey's mother's reasoning — it did seem like a solution for Casey to go home. But she also understood Casey's desire to finish the school year in Crescent Cove. Except now everyone knew Casey was pregnant. Could she live with that?

On Wednesday morning, DJ and Eliza let Lane drive them over to New Haven in his car. DJ felt like a fifth — or was it a third? — wheel as she sat in the backseat. She had tried to entice Conner to come with her at the last minute, but he said it was pointless since he had no desire to attend Yale, much less to see it. She was worried that she'd offended him simply by asking.

As they got out of the car, DJ wondered why she wanted to see Yale herself, and then she remembered it was for Grandmother's sake. The campus seemed a lot larger than Wesleyan U had been. But that didn't impress her. Nor did it impress her the way Lane and Eliza began to talk about how superior this school was to all others. If anything, it made her want to just get this over with and get out of there. But Lane insisted on giving them the whole tour. And so DJ tagged along.

"And this is the athletics department," Lane announced as they approached another set of buildings, "home of the Bulldogs." He elbowed DJ. "Bet you can't wait to check it out."

She grimaced. Mostly she was just feeling overwhelmed and eager to end the tour.

"Come on," he urged her, "let's go in."

With Lane leading the way, they wandered around the building until a man in Bulldog sweats finally asked them if they were lost.

"We'll be new students in the fall and we're just checking out the athletic department." Lane pointed to DJ. "She's the athlete."

The man smiled at DJ. "What's your sport?"

"She does it all," Eliza bragged. "She's like queen of the jock girls at our high school."

DJ felt her cheeks growing hot. "Well, not exactly."

"It's true," Lane agreed. "In fact, she was supposed to make an appointment with your athletics director, but she didn't."

"Why not?" he asked DJ.

She shrugged. "I'm not sure that Yale is the right school for me."

He looked slightly offended, but then laughed. "Now there's a line I don't hear every day."

"I'm sorry." She smiled. "It's just that I thought I'd like a small college."

"Yale is small," he said, "compared to a lot."

"I know ..."

"Would you like me to see if one of our directors is available?"

"Why not?" Lane answered for her.

"Sure," she told him. "Why not?"

"Can I get your name?" he asked. So they exchanged names, and he led them to an office with a waiting area where the three of them sat down.

"You didn't have to do this," DJ said to Lane.

"But you need to get a feel for this place," he told her, "before you completely write it off."

"DJ Lane?" the receptionist called out. DJ hopped up and went over. "Ms. Garcia said to come on back. Fourth door to the left."

So DJ hesitantly walked back and timidly knocked on the door. "Come in, come in," called out a petite, dark-haired woman. "You're DJ Lane from Crescent Cove, and I've been hoping you'd come visit."

"You know who I am?"

Ms. Garcia shook DJ's hand and held up a folder. "We've got the dirt on you, DJ."

"Dirt?"

"Ms. Jones, your basketball coach, sent us quite a package."

"Really?" DJ blinked. "I did ask my coaches to send reference letters."

188

"And they certainly did. You're quite a legend in your high school." She held up a newspaper clipping. "You saved a child's life, then won as a write-in for homecoming queen with a cast on your foot. You excel in most sports, have won best sportsmanship awards … and you've even modeled professionally?" She looked at DJ with what almost seemed like disbelief.

"Yes … that's true."

"So why wouldn't I want to see you?"

DJ made a face. "Because my grades aren't exactly stellar."

Ms. Garcia chuckled. "Well, your GPA isn't exactly top drawer. Although we did notice your grades improved during your senior year. That says a lot. And your SATs are quite impressive. So our deduction was that you were less motivated academically than you were athletically."

DJ smiled. "That's true."

Then Ms. Garcia proceeded to tell DJ all the reasons she needed to seriously consider Yale. She explained that while they didn't give athletic scholarships, they did have financial-aid packages and other incentives. After that she took DJ, Eliza, and Lane on a more complete tour of the athletic department as well as some other places where only administration was authorized to go. It was around one when she invited them to have lunch with her.

While DJ liked Ms. Garcia and was even warming up to the campus, something about it just didn't feel right to her. But to be polite, she kept this to herself as they said their good-byes, and as Ms. Garcia encouraged her to be in touch.

"Okay, DJ," Eliza said as they drove home, "I'm trying really hard not to be jealous. I mean, here I am dying to get into that school and it's like they're offering it to you on a silver platter and you're pushing it away."

"I'm not pushing it away."

"You were polite," Eliza continued, "but I could see it in your eyes. You're going to decline."

"Not necessarily," DJ protested. "I've got all these brochures and things to read, and I'll go online, and I'll talk to my grandmother."

"And then you'll tell them no," Eliza finished.

"No . . ." DJ considered this. "Then I'll pray about it."

"Do you think God is going to write the answer in the sky?" teased Lane.

"No . . . but I'm hoping he'll scribble a little something in my heart."

They laughed. But DJ wasn't kidding. She was going to pray, and she did hope that God would give her a nudge one way or the other.

**19**

*Last Dance*

AT DINNER ON WEDNESDAY, Grandmother had several announcements to make. "As you can see, Casey and her mother are not here tonight. They spent the day together in an attempt to try to figure out the best solution for Casey's . . . uh, Casey's challenge."

"Everyone knows that Casey's pregnant," DJ told her. "It's okay to say it, Grandmother."

"Fine. They're trying to work out a plan for Casey's pregnancy." Grandmother looked a little troubled. "I do hope that they will at least stay until *after* the fashion show. We're already down to eleven girls and I don't want to lose any more."

"Does that mean that you spoke to Madison?" Eliza asked nervously.

"Not yet." Grandmother scanned the faces at the table. "Which brings me to my next topic. I have an idea, a way to quietly bring Madison to justice, but it will require everyone's cooperation." Then she proceeded to tell them about a crazy plan to hold a mock court. "As you know, we're going to have our dress rehearsal for the fashion show on Friday night. But I have decided we'll be starting much earlier than planned. Four o'clock. I will invite Madison's mother and any other mothers who would like to attend." She got a slightly catty look now. "But they won't know that we're holding court. Everything will be done fairly. I've asked the general to help. What do you think?"

Everyone was onboard, including Eliza, and Grandmother made them promise not to leak the news. "I'll phone the mothers and tell them this is their invitation to a sneak peek at the fashion show. And between our court session and the dress rehearsal, I'll have Clara serve a buffet dinner." Grandmother chuckled. "Who says justice can't be fun?"


When DJ went up to the ballroom on Friday afternoon, she was surprised to see that tables and chairs were arranged into what actually looked like a makeshift courtroom. Grandmother had even managed to secure a flag, which was planted by what appeared to be the judge's desk.

"Oh, there you are," Inez called from behind a curtained-off area that DJ assumed would serve as the dressing room for that night's dress rehearsal. "Your grandmother said you'd come give me a hand."

DJ went back to see racks of clothes and Inez steaming away. "Do you want me to help steam?" she asked.

"No. I want you and some of the girls to bring Eliza's paint-stained clothes from the basement. Your grandmother had me stash them last week. You are to bring them up here. 'Exhibit A.' And hurry. It's close to four. We don't want anyone to see you."

DJ laughed. "I get it." DJ went and found Taylor and Rhiannon and they gathered up the clothes and brought them up to the ballroom, where Inez instructed them to hang them on one of the dress racks. They took their time to make sure that all the paint splatters were clearly visible.

Then they went downstairs to where Grandmother was greeting the mothers and daughters and acting like nothing out of the ordinary was about to happen. But DJ could see that Madison looked nervous. She tossed several glances DJ's way, but DJ just smiled, then looked the other way. Finally everyone was there, including the general, and Grandmother invited them all to go upstairs. "You will find that your chairs have place cards on them just like a New York show."

Of course, most of them were surprised to see the courtroom-like setup, but some didn't seem to notice, and soon everyone was in their places. Madison and her mother, as well as Tina and Jolene, were sitting on the defense side. The other mothers and some of the impartial models were in the jurors' chairs. And Eliza, DJ, and Grandmother were on the prosecution side. The general was acting as judge, and quickly bringing the courtroom to "order," which was hardly necessary since everyone was silent.

Grandmother stood. "I want to welcome you to fashion court," she told them. "We have had a fashion crime that needs to be resolved before we proceed with the fashion show." She turned toward the curtained-off area. "Will the evidence please be brought forward?"

Inez appeared with the rack of dramatic-looking, paint-splattered clothes, and almost everyone gasped. "These garments belong to Eliza Wilton and were damaged last Saturday following our modeling practice session." Grandmother went over to remove what had once been an exquisite prom dress and held it up. One of the mothers let out a loud gasp. "This was the dress that Eliza was going to wear to the prom that night." She glanced at Eliza's mother. "Is that right?"

"That's right," Mrs. Wilton said with some uncertainty.

"Do you recall the cost of this dress?"

"I purchased it in Paris with Euros, but the American equivalent would be around two thousand dollars."

Another gasp rippled through the crowd.

"The only people in the house when this crime occurred, besides my staff, who have been cleared, will now stand up." Grandmother read off the names until Jolene, Tina, Madison, Ariel, Haley, and Daisy were standing.

"What about the Carter House girls?" asked Jolene's mother.

"They all left early for Yobushi's spa," Grandmother said. "Now, of the girls standing, are there any of you who would like to make a statement?"

"I will," said Daisy. She told them that when she left, there were still several girls in the house.

"Which girls?" Grandmother asked.

"Madison, Tina, Jolene, and Ariel."

Ariel raised her hand. "I left right after Daisy and Haley. Miss Walford and I walked out together. You can ask her when she gets here."

"Thank you." Grandmother nodded. "Everyone except Madison, Tina, and Jolene may sit down. Now, would anyone else like to make a statement before we proceed?"

"I didn't do it," Jolene said quickly.

"I didn't do it either," Tina added.

"But you know who did?"

Tina and Jolene both glanced at Madison, then looked away.

"Tina and Jolene may sit down. Now, Madison," Grandmother said calmly, "is there something you'd like to tell us? Or shall I call on witnesses for the prosecution?"

Madison just stood there.

"I call DJ Lane to the witness stand," Grandmother announced.

"Okay!" Madison said loudly. "You seem to think I did this. What are you going to do about it? This isn't a real court."

"You're right. It's not a real court. Would you prefer this to be taken to a real court? The estimate of damages is nearly thirty thousand dollars."

Madison didn't answer.

"It's your choice," Grandmother said. "Abide by this jury's ruling where no criminal record is involved or take it to the next level."

"Madison," said her mother firmly, "did you do this or not?"

Madison still didn't answer.

"Would you like us to proceed with the evidence and the witnesses?" Grandmother asked.

"No!" Madison shouted.

"Then you confess?"

"Come on, Madison," Tina urged, "we saw you go in Eliza's room."

"And you're accomplices," Madison said quickly. "Right, Mrs. Carter?"

"Did your friends know you were going in there to—"

"We didn't know she was going to do *that*!" Jolene pointed to the rack of ruined clothes.

"That's true," Tina added. "She said she was going to do something with Eliza's prom dress. That's all we knew. We just waited outside."

"Guarding the door?" Grandmother asked.

They didn't answer.

"We'll deal with that later," Grandmother said. "Madison, I will ask you one last time. Did you pour paint on Eliza's clothes?"

"Yes." Madison looked down, and her mother just shook her head.

Grandmother looked at the jury. "In that case, it appears we don't need the jury." She turned to the judge. "How do you rule?"

The general looked somber as he opened an envelope and read. "We the court find Madison Dormont guilty of a fashion crime in the first degree." A few giggles escaped at this, but he continued. "The punishment for this crime will be to pay the fine of thirty thousand dollars, to be used as a donation to the Crescent Cove Boys and Girls Clubs, or to perform community service by volunteering at the Crescent Cove Boys and Girls Clubs for a total of one thousand hours or a combination of the above."

"One thousand hours?" Madison looked stunned. "What is that? Like the rest of my life?"

"There's more," the general said. "The hours of community service can be shared by friends and acquaintances of Madison, although Madison will be the responsible party."

Madison sank into her chair and groaned. The general gave the gavel a loud whack, announcing that court was adjourned.

Then Grandmother took the floor again. "I'm sorry to begin with that sad little bit of business," she told everyone, "but it seemed the easiest way to resolve this for everyone. I thank you for your patience and cooperation."

"But shouldn't Madison apologize?" asked Haley's mom.

"Yeah," agreed Daisy and several others.

"We won't force apologies," Grandmother said.

"Well, I want to apologize." Tina pointed to the rack. "I mean, I didn't realize that Madison was going to do all that. If

I'd known, I would have said something." She turned to Eliza. "I'm sorry, Eliza."

Eliza just nodded.

"I'm sorry too," Jolene said.

Eliza nodded again, but this time she spoke. "You guys really should tell DJ you're sorry. DJ gave up her dress so that I'd have something to wear. And you should apologize to Rhiannon and Taylor. They had to scramble to find something for DJ to wear. While you three were carefully putting on your prom dresses, ones you'd probably picked out long ago, we were rushing around like crazy." Eliza smiled. "But in a way it was good. It shows you who your real friends are."

Madison's mother stood now, then turned and pulled Madison to her feet. "I want to apologize for my daughter. And I will make sure she pays her fine ... one way or another."

DJ was surprised to see that Madison was crying. Whether they were tears of shame or regret, she didn't know, but DJ decided to speak up. "You know, Madison," she began slowly, "I was really hoping you were going to own up to all this and that you'd apologize, because I had decided that if you apologized, I would offer to help out by volunteering at the Boys and Girls Clubs for you. But if—"

"I'm sorry," Madison sobbed out. "I am a horrible, horrible person." She stared at the ruined clothes and then at Eliza and DJ and the others. "But you Carter House girls—you just make me so mad. You all have it so easy and you always come out on top and—"

*"We have it easy?"* Taylor said loudly. "You think we have it *easy*?"

"Right," said Casey. "I'm pregnant, and thanks to you and Jolene the whole school knows about it. That's real easy."

"And what about that online scam that someone did on Eliza recently?" DJ shot out. "That nearly destroyed her."

"And it's no secret that I was in alcohol treatment recovery," Taylor told them. "You think that was easy?"

"And my mom's been in a drug-treatment program," Rhiannon said softly. "I'm sure most of you know about that already, but it's not been real *easy*."

"And DJ's mother died tragically a couple of years ago," Grandmother said, "and she was forced to come live with her crazy old grandmother."

Kriti held up her hands. "I don't have anything too terrible," she said, "but it's not easy being Hindu ... and short amidst a bunch of tall, leggy models."

This made them all laugh. Then Grandmother invited everyone, including Madison and her mother, to a light dinner before the real dress rehearsal. Once they were downstairs, an amazing thing happened. Old petty grudges, and big ones too, seemed to be set aside. And some of the girls actually began to talk to each other. Some girls even apologized, and some shed genuine tears. Even Madison told Eliza she was sorry; whether it was sincere or not remained to be seen. But Grandmother decided to allow her to participate in the fashion show. "But do not forget you're on parole," she warned her. "One misstep and you're out." Madison shook her hand in agreement.

And in DJ's opinion, the events seemed almost miraculous.

Before long, Miss Walford arrived, and Grandmother was clapping her hands and telling the girls it was time to go upstairs and get ready. "Dylan will be here soon and we want to put our best foot forward."

The girls quickly rearranged the room from a courtroom to a fashion show, then hurried to the dressing area where several of Dylan's assistants were now on hand to help. Then Miss Walford lined the girls up, starting with Eliza.

"Dylan wanted Taylor to go first," Eliza pointed out. "And DJ was to follow."

Miss Walford scowled at Eliza. "I'm in charge of the choreography."

"But she's right," Madison said. "Dylan did have a different lineup."

Miss Walford turned toward Madison. "I'm surprised you're taking their side."

"Let's just do it Miss Walford's way," DJ said quickly. "For now."

And so they began, but the show had barely started when Dylan was yelling, "Stop! Stop!"

DJ and Taylor exchanged glances, listening from behind the curtain as Dylan demanded to know who had changed his lineup. Miss Walford explained that some of the girls had been late one day, but Dylan cut her off. "These are my clothes," he told her, "these are my models, and this is my show."

"That's right," Grandmother agreed.

"But I'm the choreographer," Miss Walford sputtered.

"And we appreciate that," Grandmother told her calmly. "But Dylan is the director. If you can't take direction from him, you —"

"I was *volunteering* to help," Miss Walford said indignantly. "But if this is how I'm treated — I don't have to take this."

DJ and Taylor peeked out in time to see her stomp out of the room. But before she was gone, Dylan clapped his hands. "All right, girls," he called out, "back to my original lineup. Taylor? DJ? Where are you?"

Before long, they were lined up according to Dylan's direction and the dress rehearsal continued. That same feeling of sisterhood and camaraderie that had begun during dinner continued, and by the time they finished their last run-through, even Dylan was impressed. "You girls work so well together," he told them. "So much better than before." He bowed. "Tomorrow's show will be a success!"

DJ wondered if some of their previous problems might have been related to Miss Walford's influence. She had so easily taken sides with her dance team girls, almost pitting them against the Carter House girls, that it sort of made sense that Madison felt entitled to take things too far. Or maybe DJ was just imagining things. Still, she thought it wouldn't do Miss Walford any harm to help Madison by volunteering at the Boys and Girls Clubs.

20

LAST DANCE

THE MOTHER'S DAY FASHION SHOW on Saturday went fairly smoothly. Oh, there were the usual bumps and blunders backstage, the occasional lost shoe or ripped seam. But no harsh words or sabotaged outfits. And no catfights. It almost gave DJ hope for what might lie ahead this summer in New York. Not that she was thinking about that much yet. She was just happy to have this particular fashion show behind her. More than that, she was happy to see everyone getting along so well. Now if only it could last the next three weeks until graduation.

Casey, thanks to the apologies and reconciliations after fashion court, had decided to remain in Crescent Cove until school ended. And she had decided to continue her pregnancy to full term. What would happen after that, Casey wasn't completely sure. Adoption was an option, but she said she wanted to take the summer to think it over.

"So you're going to stick around until graduation?" Haley asked Casey as they were getting ready before the fashion show.

"Everyone knows I'm pregnant now anyway," Casey explained as she buttoned a shirt. "What's the point in running away to hide?"

"And we're not going to give you a bad time," Madison assured her.

"Which means probably no one else will either," Tina added.

"Too bad we couldn't have been friends like this last fall," Rhiannon pointed out. "It could've saved a lot of people a lot of trouble."

"Some of us have to learn the hard way," Taylor said. "I happen to know this personally."

Grandmother had invited the mothers of the Carter House girls for a Mother's Day brunch on Sunday. All would be there except for Rhiannon's mother, since she had returned to rehab. "Hopefully, the third time's the charm," Rhiannon had told them last week when she'd heard this news from her great-aunt. Actually, it was a relief for Rhiannon since she'd been worried that something worse had happened to her MIA mom.

DJ found it interesting sitting at the table with the moms and daughters. A different kind of dynamics. Taylor and her talented jazz-singing mother. Casey and her traditional, middle-class, church-going mom. Kriti and her quiet, conservatively dressed mother. And Eliza and her fashionable, well-mannered mom. As DJ watched the mothers and daughters interacting, she saw they had moments when they seemed comfortable together and moments when they acted like strangers. And DJ wondered how she would act if her mother were here. Probably no different.

Grandmother had seated DJ and Rhiannon on either side of her. "I will play the role of your mother today," she had told them. And now she raised her glass. "I would like to make a toast to our daughters," she said loudly. The mothers raised their glasses. "To six beautiful young women with bright futures ahead—when you're rich and famous, may you always remember your mothers."

The girls laughed, and then Taylor lifted her glass. "A toast to the mothers," she said, waiting for the other girls to lift their glasses. "Here's to the mothers, you did your best and, despite everything, you might have succeeded—and if not, may you always remember we love you."

After brunch, the girls gave their mothers gifts, and DJ suddenly remembered the painting she'd gotten for her grandmother. It was underneath her bed. She excused herself and dashed up to get it, blowing the dust off the brown paper wrapping as she carried it down. She hoped that Grandmother would like it. Bradford's mom had said she might be willing to exchange it for something else if she didn't.

She found Grandmother in the kitchen, talking to Clara and Inez. "This is for you, Grandmother."

"For me?"

"Happy Mother's Day."

Grandmother looked truly stunned.

"Open it!" Inez commanded her.

They all waited while Grandmother peeled the layers of paper off. Then she just stared at the painting without saying anything.

"I know art is subjective," DJ said quickly. "But I thought maybe—"

"It's beautiful, Desiree." Grandmother turned to her with tears in her eyes. "It's too beautiful."

"Not too beautiful for you."

Grandmother just kept shaking her head. "I can't believe it."

DJ wasn't sure what to say. "For some reason it reminded me of you."

"Do you know who the artist is?" Grandmother asked.

"Just that his name is Andrew Saltzer."

Grandmother set the painting on the kitchen table and reached into her pocket for a handkerchief, carefully wiping her eyes. "Andrew Saltzer was an old friend, Desiree."

"An old beau?"

Grandmother nodded.

"You're kidding!"

"Not at all." She kept staring at the painting. "It's just unbelievable that you could've found this and bought it." She turned back to DJ. "It must've cost a fortune. Where did you get—"

"My savings."

"Oh, Desiree!"

"But you're happy I got it for you, aren't you?"

Grandmother nodded.

"And it's really beautiful. And you knew the artist."

"He was your mother's father."

DJ felt her knees go weak. "No way!"

Grandmother nodded. "Your grandfather painted that."

Inez grabbed a chair, sliding it beneath DJ and helping her to sit before she fell. "Whoa . . ." DJ just shook her head. "That's incredible."

Grandmother came over and put her arms around DJ. "And so are you. Incredible."

DJ was too stunned to respond.


The last three weeks of school passed rather peacefully and uneventfully. For the most part, the friendships between the girls who had previously been enemies continued to strengthen and grow. And several of the girls, including DJ and Taylor, donated some volunteer time (in Madison's name) at the Boys and Girls Clubs, where Madison had already become a "fixture."

DJ found herself wishing that it wasn't her last year in high school. She found it hard to believe that she'd been so opposed to Crescent Cove High one year ago. Back then she resented the small (and what she considered) stuck-up school. Now she was sad to think it was time to say good-bye. The upside of this realization was that it made her confident that her choice of college was right. DJ had thanked Yale for their kind interest and informed Wesleyan U that she'd be there in the fall. Fortunately, Grandmother backed DJ on her decision, and she was relieved that Middletown was only an hour's drive from Crescent Cove.

"You didn't go with Wesleyan for my sake, did you?" Conner had asked when she told him the good news.

"I did it for *me*," she assured him.

"Meaning I had *nothing* to do with your choice?" He looked disappointed.

"Of course you had something to do with it. You're my best friend, Conner."

"Best friend?" He looked hopeful. "Meaning I rank higher than Taylor?"

"Okay, she's my best friend too. By the way, she sent in an application to Wesleyan U last week."

"What about her big modeling career?"

"She's not sure. This summer will help her to decide."

"And did I just hear that Eliza's settling for a year of international travel in lieu of college?"

DJ chuckled. "But it's not as glamorous as it sounds. She's going with her parents, and it's mostly Third World countries. Her father joined a well-digging organization because he wants to give back."

"Cool."

DJ nodded. It was cool. And although Eliza was doing a bit of heel dragging, the good news for her was that Yale would take this into consideration when she reapplied next winter.

No one was too surprised when Kriti was tapped as valedictorian. But they were all impressed when she gave a brilliant and challenging address at graduation. As DJ listened, she regretted not spending more time getting to know Kriti this past year. But maybe it didn't matter, since all six Carter House girls had already formed a pact to stay in touch and to have regular reunions at Carter House. Naturally, this pleased Grandmother to no end.

The after-graduation party was called Last Dance and, once again, all six Carter House girls and their dates rented a stretch limo to get them to the hotel. DJ was pleased that Emery had invited Casey—and that Casey had accepted. And this time, like prom night, no alcohol was involved—they had all agreed on this in advance. Unfortunately, they knew this wasn't the case with all their high school friends.

"I can't believe this is it," Eliza said as the six girls gathered in front of the mirror in the women's restroom at the hotel. It was time to touch up their runny mascara and tear-streaked faces—remnants from graduation.

"I don't want this year to end," DJ admitted.

"Me neither." Casey grabbed a tissue and blew her nose. "I just wish I'd done it differently."

"You're going to be okay," Taylor told Casey.

"We all are," Rhiannon assured them.

Kriti nodded. "This year may have been hard at times, but it made us who we are. It made us strong."

"And it made our friendships strong," DJ said.

"Group hug!" cried Eliza. And suddenly all six of them were embracing and crying all over again.

"Good grief." A girl from graduation walked past them toward the stalls. "Maybe you guys should get a room."

They all just laughed, then Taylor called out, "Hey, if you had friends like this, you'd understand."

"We're more than just friends," DJ said seriously. "We're sisters."

"Okay, sisters," Taylor announced after they finished with their face repairs, "it's time to get out there and enjoy the Last Dance!"

And dance they did. They switched partners, visited with friends, ate food, and basically enjoyed the evening. But then the announcement came. It really was the last dance of the Last Dance.

As DJ danced with Conner, she felt a sense of bittersweet happiness. Yes, she knew it was the end of an era, and maybe she was ready to move on. But it was hard to say good-bye. She closed her eyes and thanked God for giving her such an amazing year and such great friends and, most of all, she thanked God for what was yet to come—because she knew it was going to be good!

## Share Your Thoughts

**With the Author:** Your comments will be forwarded to the author when you send them to *zauthor@zondervan.com*.

**With Zondervan:** Submit your review of this book by writing to *zreview@zondervan.com*.

## Free Online Resources at
## www.zondervan.com

**Zondervan AuthorTracker:** Be notified whenever your favorite authors publish new books, go on tour, or post an update about what's happening in their lives.

**Daily Bible Verses and Devotions:** Enrich your life with daily Bible verses or devotions that help you start every morning focused on God.

**Free Email Publications:** Sign up for newsletters on fiction, Christian living, church ministry, parenting, and more.

**Zondervan Bible Search:** Find and compare Bible passages in a variety of translations at www.zondervanbiblesearch.com.

**Other Benefits:** Register yourself to receive online benefits like coupons and special offers, or to participate in research.